"After you finish stretching, Alice," Peter continued, "you can start jogging. You have to warm up before you jog, otherwise you could get cramps and muscle spasms. James, you keep an eye on her and make sure she keeps stretching. I'll be back in a minute." Peter ran into his building.

Alice groaned. Stretching hurt. Maybe she *had* skipped too many gym classes. She was definitely out of shape.

Suddenly Alice heard a familiar voice. "Boy, if Miss Barton's whole team is like that, we're going to win easily."

Alice whirled around. Muffie Singleton stood on the sidewalk, right in front of Alice, holding a soccer ball. On either side of her were Binky Loomis and Tiffany Painter. Muffie grinned at Binky and Tiffany. "We're going to slaughter you again this year," Binky said.

"Miss Barton's doesn't have a chance," Tiffany added.

"Let's go play soccer," Muffie said. "We're wasting our time here."

Before Alice had a chance to reply, the three girls set off down the block.

"Who are they?" James asked.

"Snobs," Alice replied. She was furious. Not only were Courtney girls snobs, they were rude. She would show them!

THE AGAINST TAFFY SINCLAIR CLUB by Betsy Haynes
ALICE WHIPPLE, FIFTH-GRADE DETECTIVE
    by Laurie Adams and Allison Coudert
ALICE WHIPPLE FOR PRESIDENT by Laurie Adams and Allison
    Coudert
ALICE WHIPPLE IN WONDERLAND by Laurie Adams and
    Allison Coudert
ANNIE AND THE ANIMALS by Barbara Beasley Murphy
THE DOUBLE FUDGE DARE by Louise Ladd
THE GREAT MOM SWAP by Betsy Haynes
HEY, DIDI DARLING by S. A. Kennedy
HORSE POWER (Saddle Club #4) by Bonnie Bryant
JANET HAMM NEEDS A DATE FOR THE DANCE
    by Eve Bunting
THE KIDNAPPING OF COURTNEY VAN ALLEN &
    WHAT'S-HER-NAME by Joyce Cool
THE SARA SUMMER by Mary Downing Hahn
THIRTEEN MEANS MAGIC (Abracadabra #1)
    by Eve Becker
VALENTINE BLUES by Jeanne Betancourt
ZUCCHINI by Barbara Dana

ALICE WHIPPLE SHAPES UP

LAURIE ADAMS
and
ALLISON COUDERT

A BANTAM SKYLARK BOOK®
NEW YORK • TORONTO • LONDON • SYDNEY • AUCKLAND

RL, 3, 008–012

ALICE WHIPPLE SHAPES UP
A Bantam Skylark Book / June 1990

*Skylark Books is a registered trademark of Bantam Books, a division of
Bantam Doubleday Dell Publishing Group, Inc. Registered in U.S. Patent
and Trademark Office and elsewhere.*

ISBN 0-553-15803-1

Published simultaneously in the United States and Canada

*Bantam Books are published by Bantam Books, a division of Bantam Double-
day Dell Publishing Group, Inc. Its trademark, consisting of the words
"Bantam Books" and the portrayal of a rooster, is Registered in U.S. Patent
and Trademark Office and in other countries. Marca Registrada. Bantam
Books, 666 Fifth Avenue, New York, New York 10103.*

PRINTED IN THE UNITED STATES OF AMERICA

OPM   0 9 8 7 6 5 4 3 2 1

To Alexa, Caroline, and Polly
and to the memory of Katie

For Carole Abel and Danelle
McCafferty,
with thanks.

CONTENTS

CHAPTER ONE
ALICE IS MORTIFIED

Alice Whipple landed with a thud that echoed through the large tenth-floor gymnasium of Miss Barton's School for Girls in New York City. She heard the unmistakable sound of her classmates snickering.

"You can dismount now, Alice," said Miss Plimsoll firmly. Miss Plimsoll was the gym teacher. An Englishwoman, she was tall and thin, with crinkly gray hair, and had the faintest hint of a mustache above her upper lip. She had taught several generations of Miss Barton's girls to stand up straight, walk thirty paces with books on their heads, and generally excel at sports. Alice had never seen Miss Plimsoll in anything other than a blue blazer, a white long-sleeved shirt, and a straight, gray skirt.

"The object, Alice," Miss Plimsoll continued as she strode back and forth, "is to vault *over* the horse. Not land *on* it."

"Yes, Miss Plimsoll," Alice murmured, lifting her right leg over the leather horse to dismount. As she did so, Alice

1

noticed a distinct wobble in her thigh. Her face red, she joined her classmates who were standing by the wall. They were awaiting their turns on the exercise equipment.

"I want to remind all of you of the annual fifth-grade spring soccer match against Courtney," Miss Plimsoll told the class. "We have only six weeks to go before the match."

Courtney meant The Courtney School for Girls, Miss Barton's biggest rival. The Courtney School was less than two blocks away from Miss Barton's. The Miss Barton's girls considered the Courtney girls snobby. At Courtney, for example, the girls wore *three* different uniforms a year, a light green jumper and skirt in the fall, dark green in the winter, and pale yellow in spring. At Miss Barton's, the uniforms were dark blue all year round, and the girls tended to look scruffier than at Courtney. Still, Alice had to admit that Courtney had great team spirit. She also knew that Courtney had three particularly good fifth-grade soccer players, Muffie Singleton, Tiffany Painter, and Binky Loomis.

The annual fifth-grade soccer match was an ongoing tradition, and each year the winning team captain had her name and school engraved on a large silver cup, which had been donated by a wealthy trustee. For the past four years, Courtney had won the match and kept the cup on display in a glass case in the front hall of the school along with other trophies.

"For the first time this year," Miss Plimsoll went on, "the match will be held in the Brophy Center." Alice knew all about the Brophy Center. It was the big new sports complex, which had been built on East Ninetieth Street and was used by the neighboring schools. All the interschool games were held in the Brophy Center. It had a big field made of Astroturf with track lighting for night games. "And we expect a full house of parents and friends."

If she couldn't even vault over the horse, Alice thought, how was she going to make the soccer team? And she knew from what Miss Plimsoll said next that she wasn't.

"During the next five weeks, I am going to observe you all very carefully, and I will select the best players for the inter-school team. We will practice with a few Green-White games. And," Miss Plimsoll reminded the class, "don't forget the contest to see who can write the best cheer." It was traditional at the annual soccer match for each school to cheer for the opposite team at the beginning and at the end of the game, no matter who won.

Alice sensed the growing excitement among her classmates. There was a lot of competition between Greens and Whites; they were the school teams at Miss Barton's. As soon as a girl entered the school, she was assigned to either team and was a member of it until she graduated. And if her daughters went to Miss Barton's, they were on the same team as their mother. Alice was a Green because her mother had been a Green when she attended Miss Barton's.

Besides being divided into Greens and Whites, the fifth grade was also divided into two cliques, the Peaches and the Turnips. Not everyone was in the cliques. But the girls who were Turnips were also Whites while all the Peaches were Greens. Alice had been a Peach since fourth grade. The teachers didn't know about the Peaches and the Turnips because Miss Barton's didn't allow cliques.

Sports had never been Alice's strong point. And now she felt left out. Her best friend, Sarah Jamison, was whispering to Lydia Spaulding, another Peach. They were both good athletes. Alice watched Sarah's red curls bounce with excitement. Lydia whispered back, her long black ponytail swinging from side to side. She was an excellent runner. She loved anything that had to do with spies. She had seen all the James Bond movies. Lydia said that running was useful if you were a spy and had to escape from the Russians or the hijackers, or even from the CIA.

As Miss Plimsoll talked about the match, Alice thought about the other Peaches who would probably make the team. Hilary Jones was one. Alice and Sarah had always agreed that Hilary was a snob because all she cared about was her horse and she liked everything English. But Alice knew that horseback riding, which Hilary did three afternoons a week and on weekends, was a good way to stay in shape. It didn't do your thighs any harm either. Wing Chu was another Peach who would make the team. She was a serious gymnast. She could never come to your birthday party if you had it on a Friday afternoon because she always went to her gymnastics class. Wing Chu didn't have one single wobble in *her* thigh.

Marina was standing on the other side of Sarah, and Alice saw the two of them talking. *Where is Sarah's loyalty?* Alice thought. Marina was a Peach and a Green, but you could never count on her. All she cared about were boys. She thought she was so great because she was tall and the only fifth grader who wore a bra.

"Pssst! Sarah!" Alice heard Marina whispering. "Miss Plimsoll said to invite friends. That means we can invite *boys* to the soccer match." Marina played soccer in Central Park on weekends; but Alice knew that she only did it to meet the boys who played.

Miss Plimsoll called out the girls' names for their turns on the vaulting horse; but Alice was more interested in hearing the whispered conversations around her than in watching her classmates jump over a vaulting horse.

She heard Donna Ellington, the leader of the Turnips whispering to her best friend Jane. "Well, we know *one* person who won't make the team." Donna had run against Alice for class president, and Jane had been her running mate. Alice thought Donna was the preppiest girl in the class. She had at least six Benetton sweaters, and she always wore matching socks. Jane smirked and stared at Alice through her thick tortoiseshell glasses.

That was the last straw! First the vaulting horse, then the Peaches ignoring her, and now sneering from the Turnips. Alice would have to do something about it. She knew that her record in gym was not great. Only a week ago she had come in last in the thirty-yard dash and just yesterday she had hit the volleyball into the net every time it came to her. At the last Green-White softball game, Alice had struck out each time she was up at bat, and in the badminton tournament, she split her racket hitting the net post when swinging at the birdie. Miss Plimsoll had not been at all pleased. She believed in taking good care of the sports equipment. Alice remembered when Sarah had been sitting on the treadmill taking a short rest. Miss Plimsoll made her stay after school and write a hundred times, "It is dangerous to sit on the treadmill, even when it is turned off." And Sarah was *good* at gym.

Alice was thinking hard. Hadn't Helen Keller learned to read and write and speak even though she was blind and deaf? The class had read her biography in language arts. And what about Theodore Roosevelt? They had studied him in their history unit on the American presidents. He was never much good at sports as a child. But he became a great athlete and a big-game hunter when he grew up. And hadn't Cynthia

Ryan's math facts improved after her parents got her a tutor? Obviously you could be good at something if you really wanted to and made a special effort. Alice still had five weeks before Miss Plimsoll chose the interschool team.

Alice made a decision. She was tired of being bad at sports. And it was not at all good for her image as leader of the Peaches. She felt that she was losing ground with her friends. Alice resolved that not only would she get into shape, but she would also make the interschool soccer team and be a credit to the Peaches. In fact, she intended to win the cheer-writing contest as well!

CHAPTER TWO

MR. WHIPPLE LEARNS TO COOK

"**I**s Daddy cooking again?" Beatrice poked her head into the living room. Beatrice Whipple was Alice's younger sister and a first grader at Miss Barton's. Both Beatrice and Alice had short blond hair and blue eyes. She looked a lot like Alice. The Whipple family lived on the second floor of a small apartment building on East Eighty-eighth Street between Park and Madison avenues in New York City.

"Yes, dear," Mrs. Whipple replied. "We're very lucky that Daddy is learning to cook." Mrs. Whipple usually did the cooking, but she had sprained her ankle when she twisted her foot in a pothole as she crossed a street. There were a lot of potholes in the New York City streets. The doctor told her to stay off the foot and keep it propped up on an ice pack. Mary Whipple was a part-time reading teacher, but because of her foot she hadn't been to work for several days. Instead she took advantage of her enforced vacation to read the books she usually didn't have time for. Gerald Whipple took care of the house and the cooking after work. He was a banker.

Beatrice thought of the meals they had been eating lately. Icky stir-fried dishes from the Chinese cookbook, disgusting pie with spinach and cheese from the Greek cookbook, and yucky herring from the Norwegian cookbook.

"You and Alice should set the table now," her mother said.

"Alice!" Beatrice yelled. "You have to help me set the table!"

Alice was in her room studying. She closed her book and joined Beatrice. As they walked into the kitchen, Mr. Whipple announced cheerfully, "Dinner is almost ready."

The kitchen was filled with smoke. "Daddy, I think something's burning," Alice said. "What are we having?"

"Tonight I'm making your favorite dinner. It's from *The American Easy Recipe Cookbook.*"

After Alice and Beatrice had set the dining room table, Mrs. Whipple hopped from the living room into the dining room on her crutches. She sat down and propped up her sprained ankle on an empty chair.

"Here we are, everyone." Mr. Whipple entered in a cloud of smoke, carrying a large tray with several dishes and platters on it.

Alice and Beatrice sat down. Alice had a book on her lap, and she kept glancing from it to the tray.

"Alice, you're not allowed to read at the table," Beatrice reminded her.

"Shut up, Beatrice! I'm not reading, I'm checking a reference."

"Reference?" her mother said. "Reference to what?"

"Nutrition," Alice replied. "We're studying nutrition in our science unit. Our assignment is to review what we eat and to make a list of all the vitamins and minerals and food groups we have in a week. We also have to keep track of how many calories we eat and burn up."

With a flourish, Mr. Whipple placed the dishes one by one on the table.

"What's that, Daddy?" Alice asked, pointing to a large blue covered dish.

"That," said her father as he lifted the lid, "is a tuna fish casserole."

"Yuck," Beatrice said. She hated tuna fish.

"But Daddy," Alice said, "tuna fish has mercury in it. Do you know what mercury does to you? It makes your teeth and hair fall out."

"I guess Grandpa ate a lot of tuna fish," Beatrice observed.

"Tuna fish is fish," Mr. Whipple said firmly. "And fish is an excellent source of protein." He served the casserole. "And furthermore, the macaroni in this casserole is a good carbohydrate. Add that to your list of food types, Alice."

"But you've made corn on the cob, Daddy," Alice said. "That makes *two* carbohydrates. And the corn is dripping with butter. Butter is an animal fat, and animal fat is the worst kind of fat. You should eat vegetable fat instead. Besides, you're supposed to have *one* thing from every food group, not two. Carbohydrates turn into sugar when you digest them. We tested carbohydrates for sugar in science today. They turn green or orange when you add Benedict's solution to them. How would you like to eat orange macaroni and green corn? Also, too much sugar is bad for you."

"Peter and James eat a lot of chocolate," Beatrice pointed out. "Chocolate has tons of sugar, and there's nothing wrong with Peter and James. They never even get sick."

Peter and James Hildreth were friends from across the street. They attended the local public school. Peter was in the fifth grade and James was a first grader.

Alice brightened up as her father handed around a plate of sliced tomatoes. "I hope you washed those tomatoes, Daddy. They spray tomatoes with pesticides."

"I'm sure your father washed the tomatoes, Alice," Mrs. Whipple said.

"I don't see any greens, Daddy," Alice went on. "Green vegetables have vitamin B_2, which is good for your skin and your eyes, and niacin, which helps your circulation and lowers your cholesterol. Our teacher said the latest experiments show that niacin keeps you from losing your appetite."

"*You* don't have to worry about losing *your* appetite, Alice," her sister said.

"Oh, be quiet," Alice said.

"It's good to have a healthy appetite," Mrs. Whipple informed Beatrice.

Alice hadn't finished discussing green vegetables. "Popeye eats spinach. Why don't you make some spinach sometime, Daddy?"

"We *had* spinach," Beatrice said. "In the horrible Greek pie."

Mr. Whipple decided not to discuss the greens. "Now for your very favorite," he said enthusiastically as he lifted the lid off the last dish.

Alice and Beatrice leaned forward and peered into it.

"Oh, boy!" Beatrice said. "Your cooking is really improving. I love hot dogs with cheese wrapped in bacon."

"But, Daddy," Alice said, "according to our science book, even the best hot dogs are at least ten percent bones, gristle, and skin."

"*Whose* bones, gristle, and skin?" Beatrice demanded.

"Cows and pigs and chickens and turkeys, depending on what the hot dogs are made of, stupid. And hot dogs have nitrites," Alice continued, "which are preservatives and can give you cancer. And the bacon is full of sodium, which makes you retain water. And you used American cheese. American cheese is processed—"

"That's enough, Alice!" Mr. Whipple declared. "You were perfectly happy with hot dogs when your mother made them two weeks ago."

"That was before Alice went on her diet," Beatrice announced. "She's too fat to get on the soccer team. Maybe she should go to a fat farm and drink carrot juice for two weeks. Then she'd be happy to eat hot dogs."

It annoyed Alice that Beatrice never seemed to gain weight even though she ate quite a lot. Alice had never really lost all her baby fat, and Beatrice never seemed to have had any in the first place. It wasn't fair, Alice thought. To make things worse, Beatrice was a natural athlete. She didn't even have to *try* to do well in gym.

"You know, Beatrice," Mr. Whipple said, "you don't necessarily have to be thin to be good at sports. Some very famous athletes have been overweight. Babe Ruth, for example, was one of the greatest baseball players of all time. By today's standards he was definitely overweight. And Jack Nicklaus was very heavy when he was young, which didn't prevent him from being a great golfer. And don't forget JoAnne Carner; they call her 'big mama' on the golf circuit." Mr. Whipple was an avid golfer.

"Really, Gerald," Mary Whipple interrupted. "I think you're missing the point. Alice is *not* fat. And she can be a good athlete if she wants to. Perhaps she just needs to take gym a bit more seriously."

"If Alice didn't get so many gym excuses from Mrs. Tully, she'd get more practice," Beatrice said, grinning smugly at Alice.

Mrs. Tully was the school nurse at Miss Barton's. She had a broad, friendly smile and a cheerful disposition. Whether the girls had a sniffle, a bruise, or an emotional crisis, Mrs. Tully could always be counted on to be available and very sensible. Her office had a brightly colored sign over the door that read, A PLACE WHERE STRENGTH IS REGAINED AND HEALTH IS RENEWED. Inside, Mrs. Tully kept bowls of cinnamon bark and vases of flowers to freshen the air. Bunk beds accommodated the girls who needed a rest. Mrs. Tully's office was easily the most lavishly decorated room in the entire school and was particularly busy during gym classes or when a big test was coming up.

Before Alice could respond, Beatrice said, "The whole fifth grade is trying to get on the interschool soccer team to play against Courtney. Everyone was talking about it on the school bus today. And Alice doesn't have a chance." Beatrice took a big bite of her hot dog. "Daddy," she said, "if Alice isn't going to eat her hot dog, I want it. Alice can have my tomatoes."

Alice stared gloomily at the tomatoes. Things were not going well. How could she be expected to stick to a healthy diet when everyone in the whole world ate nothing but junk food? And if she didn't eat healthy food, how was she going to shape up and make the interschool soccer team?

CHAPTER THREE

CARROTS AND CELERY STICKS

The next day Alice, Sarah, and Lydia were sitting at their favorite corner table in the school cafeteria. Alice unpacked her lunch. It consisted of three celery sticks, three carrot sticks, four slices of green pepper, one tomato, a small piece of cheddar cheese, and one orange. She had bought a small carton of skim milk. Lydia and Sarah had gotten hamburgers and chocolate milk shakes from the cafeteria counter. They stared at Alice's lunch.

Hilary rushed up to join their table and plunked down her brown and tan Gucci bag. Alice knew that meant that Hilary had brought in another fantastic lunch prepared by her cook. Hilary refused to carry a normal Snoopy or Batman lunch box like everyone else. She said they lacked distinction.

At Miss Barton's a student could bring her own lunch if she had a note from her doctor. Alice had persuaded Mrs. Tully to write a note saying that she was on a special athlete's diet. Alice wondered what Hilary's doctor said in his note. Maybe she was on a diet to get fat, which she never did, Alice thought enviously.

Alice pretended not to notice as Hilary unpacked her bag. But with each piece of food, Alice's mouth watered just a little bit more. Two cups of cashew nuts, a container of olives, a wedge of soft creamy Brie cheese, special English crackers, eight chocolate chip cookies, and chocolate milk that stayed cold in the thermos.

Alice nibbled on a carrot. She made a mental count of the calories spread out in front of Hilary. There were at least three hundred calories in the cashews and three hundred in the Brie. English crackers, or biscuits, were loaded with sugar, and they were either made with butter or lard, both of which were animal fats. And what about the cookies and the chocolate milk? Alice didn't really know about chocolate milk, but she was sure that her calorie book said that one single square of a Hershey's bar had fifty calories. There probably were eight or ten chocolate chips to a square of a Hershey's bar, and there were a lot of chocolate chips in those cookies. Probably they were homemade, and then you had to count the batter. If they were homemade, they would have butter and flour and sugar in them—

"Alice!" Hilary interrupted her calculations. "What's the matter with you?" She tossed her straight brown hair back over her shoulders. "Don't you want to taste my lunch?"

Alice was jolted back to the conversation. Hilary held out a handful of cashews.

"Oh. No, thanks, Hilary. I couldn't."

"What do you mean 'couldn't'? That's not like you, Alice.

Maybe you should go see Mrs. Tully. I bet you're getting sick."
Hilary popped the nuts into her mouth.

"I bet she's on a diet," Lydia said with her mouth full of
hamburger.

"My father knows a lot about diet foods," Sarah added.
"He says you have to be careful when you go on a diet. You
never know what they put into diet foods." Sarah's father was
in the advertising business.

"I am *not* on a diet," protested Alice as she crossed her
fingers under the table. She couldn't bring herself to admit that
she was worried about getting into shape. "I've just been
thinking about what Mr. Moffet said about the importance of
good nutrition." Mr. Moffet was the fifth grade science teacher.
"Do you realize"—Alice shook her carrot stick at Hilary—"that
cashew nuts are loaded with oil?"

Alice was glad to see Hilary return the nuts to her plate.
"And just look at that cheese. Brie is *soft* cheese. And soft
cheese is full of cholesterol." Alice was really warming to her
subject. "Every time you bite into that cheese, your body ab-
sorbs tons of cholesterol. And each bit of cholesterol sticks to
your arteries and clogs them up. That's how you get heart at-
tacks."

"My father says you should eat margarine. It has less cholesterol than butter." Sarah slurped her chocolate milk shake.

"There's no butter in my lunch, Sarah." Hilary delicately bit
into an olive.

"Those olives," Alice continued, "are full of salt. Salt's bad
for your heart too. And you don't know how long olives have
been in the store before you buy them. They float around in
preservatives until you open the jar. Just like the dead frogs in
the biology lab—pickled!"

Hilary put down the half-eaten olive and picked up a chocolate chip cookie.

"Sugar, Hilary!" Alice turned to Sarah and Lydia. They had nearly finished their hamburgers, and their plates were smeared with catsup. "Didn't any of you hear what Mr. Moffet said about sugar? Or red meat? He said that Americans eat much too much red meat. And catsup is practically all sugar. Same for milk shakes. Your teeth will turn brown, rot, and fall out. You'll have to chew with your gums. Have you ever tried to chew with your gums? Besides, sugar makes you hyperactive."

"I don't think you have to worry about that, Alice. You can't even get over the vaulting horse." Hilary snickered.

Alice ignored Hilary and nibbled on a celery stick. *At least you can't get fat on celery sticks,* she thought. In fact, it took more calories to chew and digest a celery stick than the celery stick had to begin with.

"Listen, Alice. We're trying to finish our lunch." Lydia pushed her half-empty milk shake glass to the edge of her tray. "Let's change the subject."

Lydia turned to Sarah and Hilary. "Who do you think is going to make the soccer team? We want to make sure there's a majority of Peaches. But I'm afraid the Turnips may outnumber us."

Lydia took a sheet of paper from her notebook, which was on the empty chair next to her. She plucked a Miss Barton's pencil from her uniform pocket. "The three of us will certainly be on the team." Lydia did not look at Alice.

Alice pretended not to be interested as Lydia made a list.

"Don't forget Wing Chu," Sarah said. "She's awfully good at soccer. And Marina. She's so tall they'll probably put her on too."

Lydia added their names.

"That's only five Peaches," Hilary said. "There are eleven on a soccer team. We need at least one more Peach."

"How about Toni and Caroline?" Sarah asked.

It was not lost on Alice that her name had not even been mentioned.

"Toni and Caroline are not as good as Sandra and Ellen; and they're Turnips." Lydia chewed her eraser as she considered the options. "Of the Turnips, Cynthia, Tracey, and Ellen are sure to be chosen. Even though they're the shortest girls in the class, they're fast runners. Ellen won the sprint last week. And of course Donna and Jane. Donna's the best athlete in the class and Jane is almost as good as Sarah." Lydia wrote down some more names. "This is the situation as of now." Lydia held up her list.

Peaches	Turnips
Sarah	Sandra
Hilary	Ellen
Lydia	Cynthia
Wing Chu	Tracey
Marina	Donna
	Jane

Alice Whipple was not on the list.

"Maybe," Sarah suggested, "if we coached Toni and Caroline, they could be as good as Sandra and Ellen. Especially if they practiced. Toni won the badminton tournament, and Caroline plays tennis every week."

And Sarah was supposed to be her best friend, Alice thought. You couldn't trust anyone anymore.

Alice tried one more thing. "Aren't any of you interested in the cheer? I think we should write a cheer together so we can win the contest."

"Please, Alice. Be serious. We have more important things to concentrate on." Lydia slurped the last of her milk shake.

Sarah finished her hamburger and wiped her mouth.

"That's a good idea, Sarah," said Hilary, referring to the coaching. She zipped up her Gucci bag. "Let's get them and go up to the gym. We have twenty minutes of lunch period left. If we start practicing right now, we'll have six weeks. A lot can happen in six weeks."

Still talking, Sarah, Lydia, and Hilary rose from the table. Sarah and Lydia took their trays and empty dishes to the conveyor belt, which returned them to the kitchen. Hilary slung her bag over her shoulder. Alice watched them leave. They hadn't even noticed that she was still sitting there.

Alice was depressed and worried. The whole class had gone crazy. All they talked about was the soccer game. If she didn't do something soon, they would forget that she was the leader of the Peaches.

Alice stared at the remainder of her lunch. Only the orange was left. *Oh well*, she reassured herself. *At least if you eat oranges you get plenty of vitamin C. Vitamin C keeps you from getting scurvy.* People with scurvy had no energy. You couldn't be a great soccer player if you had scurvy. And Alice Whipple had every intention of becoming quite a good soccer player. Good enough to make the interschool team.

She was glad that Sarah had mentioned coaching. Coaching, Alice thought, was clearly the solution to her problem. She would talk to Peter when she got home.

CHAPTER FOUR
ALICE FINDS A COACH

On Saturday morning Alice peered across the street from her kitchen window. According to her Swatch, it was exactly 8:25 AM. *They'll be coming out any minute,* she thought. Alice waited. And there they were. Right on the dot of 8:30, Peter and James Hildreth emerged from their apartment building. They had been friends with Alice and Beatrice since they had moved into the neighborhood five years ago. Both boys had brown hair and lots of freckles. Alice thought they probably hadn't even bothered to comb their hair that morning because it looked very messy. She could tell they were in a hurry.

Alice wrote a note to her mother, telling her she was outside. She stuck it on the refrigerator with a dinosaur magnet. Then she quickly pulled on a green Miss Barton's sweatshirt with white Gothic lettering and left the apartment. Her parents and Beatrice were still asleep. Alice wasn't usually up and dressed so early on Saturday morning either, but she had an important mission to accomplish. She closed the front door of her building and stepped into the street as Peter and James disappeared around the corner. She knew they would be right back.

Every Saturday morning, Mr. and Mrs. Hildreth gave Peter and James their weekly allowance. And every Saturday morning the boys sped off to Zorba's, the local coffee shop, to buy chocolate bars. Zorba's opened early, even on Saturdays. Alice considered what she would say. She knew that Peter had to be approached in just the right way. She strolled slowly toward the corner and bumped into James, who wasn't looking where he was going. He was concentrating on unwrapping a Kit Kat.

"Why, hi, James. Hi, Peter. What a surprise!" Alice decided to appear nonchalant.

"How come you're up so early?" Peter asked Alice. "What do you want?"

"I bet she wants our chocolate," James said matter-of-factly.

"Is that what you want, Alice? Because if it is, you aren't getting any. We have to wait all week for our allowance."

"Please, Peter. What makes you think I want *my* teeth to fall out?"

"Your *teeth*? You never worried about your teeth before."

"Before was different. This is now."

"What's the difference between before and now?"

"Before was before," Alice said. "Now I'm in training."

"In training?" Peter looked as if he didn't believe her. "*You?* Training for what?"

Alice drew herself to her full height, which was more than Peter's. Peter was short for his age; the top of his head reached just to Alice's eyes. But her mother always said he would be tall when he grew up because his grandparents were tall. "I'm in training for the big annual soccer match between Miss Barton's and Courtney."

Peter hooted. "Soccer! You! Ha! You can't kick a ball to save your life. Besides, you hate sports."

Alice was having trouble controlling her anger. "That was before, Peter. This is a very important match. The honor of Miss Barton's is at stake."

"'The honor of Miss Barton's,'" Peter mimicked. He and James went to the local public school, and he hated it when Alice talked like that. "And anyway, that's girls' soccer. It's not serious soccer."

"Oh, yes it is. It's very serious. Miss Barton's has lost the match for every one of the last four years. Ever since I've been in *first grade.* That means Courtney has had the trophy all that time. This year I want to make sure that Miss Barton's wins and gets back the trophy."

"But Alice," Peter protested, "you're terrible at soccer."

"Yeah." James finally stopped eating long enough to say something. He licked the remains of the Kit Kat off his fingers. "When we tried to play with you last summer, you missed the ball every time."

"Quiet, James," Alice said. "I do realize," she continued and stared at Peter, "that there's always room for improvement."

"You can say that again."

"Which is why I got up early this morning and came out here to find you."

"Oh?"

"Yes. I have a plan."

"Uh-oh." Peter was decidedly suspicious. When Alice had

a plan, he knew that it usually meant trouble for him. "What kind of a plan?"

"You'd have to help, of course."

"Help do what?"

"Listen, Peter. I think it would be good experience for you to be a soccer coach. It so happens that I need a soccer coach."

"Soccer coach? But I'm already the captain of my class soccer team."

"Right! A good captain has to be a good coach. He has to run the whole team. He has to know the weak points and the strong points of each of his players. He has to know when to make a substitution. He has to understand each position. He has to—"

"Okay, Alice," Peter interrupted. "But I've got enough to do with the team. I don't want to be your coach."

Alice was not going to give up. "Think what a big favor I'd be doing you."

"*You'd* be doing *me* a favor?"

"Yes."

Peter frowned.

"Don't listen to her, Peter," James said. "We've got lots of boys we can play soccer with."

"Of course, I could probably arrange for you both to come to the soccer match," Alice went on. "It's going to be held at the Brophy Center on a real Astroturf field."

"Astroturf isn't real, Alice. It's synthetic. I prefer grass. Our school plays on grass."

"*You* won't be playing, Peter. You'll be watching."

"Why would I want to watch girls play soccer?"

Alice was getting desperate. Nothing was working. "Listen, Peter. Just think about it, okay? You're absolutely right. I *am* terrible at sports. That's the whole point. If you could teach me to be good enough to get on the team, you'd have a great reputation."

Peter grew thoughtful.

"She's going to get you in trouble," James warned.

Peter ignored his brother. Finally he replied to Alice. "Okay," he said slowly. "You're my friend, so I'll help you. But training isn't going to be easy. It means hard work, lots of exercise, and no cheating on your diet. That means no chocolate."

"I know all that. And I'm completely serious. In fact, I'm ready to start now."

"Now?" Peter raised his eyebrows doubtfully. "Well, I guess we *could* begin. Tell you what"—he perked up—"you stay here and stretch while I go get my stopwatch."

"Stretch? Stopwatch?"

"Well, yes. You said you were serious."

"But I don't know what you mean by stretching."

"Don't they teach you anything in that sissy school?"

"Listen, Peter, coaches are supposed to encourage their players, not insult them."

"Okay, Alice. Here's what you do. Lean against the wall, like this, and put one leg straight out behind you. Then stretch your calf muscles." Peter leaned against the wall of his building and demonstrated. "This is good for your heel cords too."

"Heel cords?" James asked.

"Yes. Heel cords are on the back of your heels. They're your Achilles tendons, and they're very important for jogging."

Alice knew what an Achilles heel was because she had read about Achilles in her language arts unit on Greek mythology. When Achilles was a baby, his mother held him by the heels and dipped him into a river to make him immortal. Only his heels didn't get wet so they were his vulnerable spots. Later, during the Trojan War, he was killed by a poisoned arrow, which hit his heel. Alice had every intention of strengthening her heel cords.

"After you finish stretching, Alice," Peter continued, "you can start jogging. You have to warm up before you jog, otherwise you could get cramps and muscle spasms. James, you keep an eye on her and make sure she keeps stretching. I'll be back in a minute." Peter ran into his building.

Alice groaned. Stretching hurt. Maybe she *had* skipped too many gym classes. She was definitely out of shape.

Suddenly Alice heard a familiar voice. "Boy, if Miss Barton's whole team is like that, we're going to win easily."

Alice whirled around. Muffie Singleton stood on the sidewalk, right in front of Alice, holding a soccer ball. She was wearing orange sweatpants and a pink long-sleeved T-shirt. On either side of her were Binky Loomis and Tiffany Painter. Muffie grinned at Binky and Tiffany. "We're going to slaughter you again this year," Binky said, adjusting the waistband of her black bicycle shorts.

"Miss Barton's doesn't have a chance," Tiffany added.

"Let's go play soccer," Muffie said. "We're wasting our time here."

Before Alice had a chance to reply, the three girls set off down the block.

"Who are they?" James asked.

"Snobs," Alice replied. She was furious. Not only were Courtney girls snobs, they were rude. She would show them. Alice turned back to the wall, leaned over, and resumed stretching her right leg.

"She didn't do her left leg yet," James reported as Peter returned.

"Now do your left leg, Alice," Peter said.

Alice stretched her left leg.

"Now your hamstrings."

"My what?"

"Hamstrings, Alice, the muscles in the back of your legs. Like this." Peter bent over and touched his toes. "Be sure to bend your knees slightly while you lean over, otherwise you could hurt your back."

Alice bent over, being careful about her knees. But she could barely reach midway down her calf, let alone all the way to her toes.

"Mmmm," Peter said thoughtfully. "You're going to need a lot of work, Alice. Do that ten times."

Alice did so. Each time she reached a little farther so that by the tenth time she was down to her ankles.

"Good," Peter said, noting her progress. "You'll start with three laps around the block. When I say go, you run. Don't run too fast at first. Remember, racehorses aren't supposed to speed up until the last minute. And don't forget to breathe. Beginners always forget to breathe."

Alice didn't think she would forget to breathe. She took a deep breath and started off toward Madison Avenue.

Peter pushed the start knob on his stopwatch. "You could go a little faster than that," he called out.

Four minutes later Alice rounded the corner of Park Avenue and Eighty-eighth Street and arrived back at the entrance to Peter's building, which was halfway down the block. Peter and James were lounging against the brightly polished bronze fire hydrant protruding from the brick wall. They were chewing. Alice stopped, panting.

"Don't stop, Alice. That's only one lap. And it took you too long. Four minutes is too long. Most people can *walk* around the block in four minutes."

"But—" Alice protested.

"Listen. Do you or do you not want me to be your coach? Because if you do, then you're going to have to follow the rules."

Alice took another deep breath and started out again.

Six minutes later, Peter was feeling very impatient. James had eaten another bar of chocolate.

"Hi, Peter. Hi, James," called Sarah Jamison. She was on roller skates.

"Hi, Sarah. What're you doing here?"

"I'm on my way to the park. I'm meeting some of the Peaches, and we're going to practice soccer."

"That's funny," James said. "Alice is practicing too."

"She is?" Sarah looked puzzled. "What for?"

"We're helping Alice get in shape for the interschool soccer match," Peter explained. "She needs a lot of help."

"That's really nice of you, Peter. It would be great if Alice *could* make the team. But I don't see her practicing. Where is she?"

"She's running around the block. At least I thought she was. I don't know what's happened to her." Peter checked his watch. "She's been gone seven and a half minutes."

"Even Alice should be able to get around the block in seven and a half minutes," Sarah said.

"Maybe she fell and can't get up," Peter suggested.

"Maybe she sprained her ankle and broke her leg," James said. "Or maybe she got kidnapped by a man in a stretch limousine."

"Don't be silly, James."

"Well, if you're so smart, you figure it out. I'm going home to get my roller skates."

"Wait a minute, James. That's a good idea. Get your skates, and we'll divide up into two search parties and look for Alice."

James went inside and came out again with the skates.

"Okay, James," Peter said. "I'll jog down to Madison, and you and Sarah skate around the block in the other direction, until we meet up. We're sure to find Alice that way."

They set off at once. Peter ran into James and Sarah at the corner of Eighty-eighth Street and Madison.

"Well?" Sarah began. "Did you see her?"

"No," Peter said.

"Uh-oh." Sarah stared past Peter.

"What is it?"

"Look there." Sarah pointed at the window of Zorba's Coffee Shop. "Follow me."

Seated at the counter, her back to the window, was Alice Whipple. She was concentrating so hard on her black cow, a mixture of Coca-Cola and vanilla ice cream, that she didn't see Peter, James, and Sarah until they were right behind her.

"Alice!" Peter said in a very loud voice. "What do you think you're doing?"

Alice whirled around. "Peter, Sarah! What are *you* doing here?"

"Looking for you." Peter sounded very annoyed. "You're supposed to be running around the block. This is absolutely against the rules. This is absolutely *not* the way to get in shape. And I absolutely resign as your coach."

"Listen, Peter," Alice said quickly. "I ran this far, and then I realized that I needed sugar. Remember, Sarah, Mr. Moffet told us that sugar gives you energy?"

"You don't need energy," Sarah said. "All you're doing is eating."

"Peter and James have been eating chocolate all morning."

"*They* are not in training. They're already in shape. And they're good soccer players. The Peaches need good soccer players. It's too bad Peter and James aren't Peaches."

"That's exactly why I want Peter to be my coach. I need him to inspire me."

"Inspiration isn't enough, Alice. You have to work hard and practice. You can't just sit around and drink sodas. You'll never make the team this way." Sarah looked at the clock on the coffee shop wall. "I have to go practice." Sarah skated outside before Alice could say a word.

Alice was even more worried than before. Things were going from bad to worse. If only Sarah hadn't found her at Zorba's. Now Sarah would never believe that Alice could shape up in time to make the team. And if she didn't make the team, she might never be Peach leader again. In fact, she might not even *be* a Peach.

Peter could see that Alice was upset.

"If you really want to shape up, you'd better do what I say," he declared. "Or forget it."

Alice was really tired, but she agreed to follow Peter's instructions. She had an idea. "Have you ever done yoga, Peter? Mrs. Tully says yoga is good for your muscles. And it helps you relax."

"Yes, but it doesn't help you *move*. You have to *move* when you play soccer. You don't play soccer in a sitting position while you're eating. And you're not supposed to relax either. You're supposed to be alert. If you're not alert when you play soccer, you might get hit in the head by the ball, or trip over, or bump into, another player. You don't want to make extra penalties for your team, do you?"

Alice definitely did not want to make extra penalties. She was going to lead her team to victory.

"Let's get back to work," Peter said.

Alice paid for her black cow and hopped off the counter stool. She followed Peter and James back to their building.

Ten minutes later, Alice collapsed on the front stoop of the building next to Peter's. "I can't run any more," she gasped. She was breathing heavily, and her face was bright red.

"That was better, Alice. You're making progress."

"Is Alice all right, Peter? She isn't saying anything." James stared at Alice.

"She's fine. That's what happens to you when you get out of shape. It takes time to increase your stamina. You have to do it gradually."

"What's stamina?" James wanted to know.

"It's like energy. Alice is breathing hard because she has a high pulse rate. Your pulse rate goes down when you're in good shape. Long-distance runners have a very low pulse rate. In fact, they carry a special card in case they have an accident and get taken to the hospital so the doctors won't think they're in shock. Your pulse rate goes down a lot when you're in shock."

Alice did not have the remotest intention of being taken to the hospital. "I think you should give me some chocolate, Peter." Alice had stopped panting. "I need energy. I feel faint."

Peter could tell Alice was faking. She was breathing normally, and her face was back to its regular color.

"No snacks," he said firmly. "You should ask your mother to get you some Gatorade next time she goes to the store. Gatorade restores the minerals you lose when you sweat. It was invented for the football teams in Florida; that's why it's called Gatorade, after the Florida alligators. Now it's time for your jumps. James, go get the jump rope. It's in the skate box next to the front door."

James ran inside.

Alice groaned.

James came right out again carrying the rope.

"Okay, Alice. Take it slowly at first. Jumping rope is a good aerobic exercise, which will improve your breathing and your heart rate. Jump at your own pace for three minutes. Then you can rest until tomorrow. When you get home, be sure to put ice on your sore muscles for twelve minutes. Tonight take a hot bath." Peter handed Alice the rope and set his stopwatch to 3. He pushed the button. "Begin now."

"Mommy, come look!" Beatrice pressed her nose against the kitchen window.

"I can't, Beatrice. I have to stay off my ankle." Mrs. Whipple and Beatrice had had breakfast, and Mrs. Whipple was on the living room sofa with her ankle propped up on three pillows. "What are you looking at?"

"It's Alice. She was running around the block. Now she's jumping rope. Peter and James are timing her."

"Alice running? Jumping rope? Being timed? Are you sure it's Alice? I guess I can get up to see that." Mrs. Whipple hopped to the living room window.

CHAPTER FIVE

A NOT-SO-
PERFECT KICK

"**W**hy do we have to cheer for the other team, Mrs. Parker?" Hilary asked. "They don't do that in English soccer matches." It was Monday morning, ten days after the soccer match had been announced.

"It's a tradition at Miss Barton's, Hilary. We always cheer the other team during interschool games. It's a question of sportsmanship." Fifth grade was the first year for interschool matches at Miss Barton's.

Mrs. Parker was the cheerful, slightly plump fifth-grade homeroom teacher. She also taught history, which was the first class on Monday. Sometimes homeroom topics and history ran together.

"Remember," Mrs. Parker continued, "it doesn't matter if you win or lose, it's the effort that counts."

Alice raised her hand. "If that's true, Mrs. Parker, then why do only the best athletes and students get all the prizes?"

"That's a good question, Alice. It's important to reward excellence. But sportsmanship is also very important. That's why at Miss Barton's we have prizes for students who have improved the most during the year and for students who have shown the most effort. Athletics are a crucial part of your education, girls. Do any of you remember what *Mens sana in corpore sano* means?"

"I do." Wing Chu's hand shot up. "It's Latin for 'A sound mind in a sound body.'"

"Very good, Wing Chu." Mrs. Parker wrote the phrase on the blackboard and pointed to each word. "*Mens* means 'mind' and *sana* means 'sound' or 'healthy.' The word *sanitary* comes from *sana*. Together they mean 'a sound mind.' *Corpore* means 'body' so *corpore sano* means 'a sound body.'"

"*Corpore* must be where the word *corpse* comes from," said Lydia, who loved murder mysteries as well as spy novels.

"That's right, Lydia. It is also the Latin word from which we get *corporation,* which is an organization of bodies, and *corporeal,* meaning having to do with the body. *Corpulent* means 'having a fat body.'"

Both Marina and Hilary glanced at Alice and snickered.

Alice looked the other way.

"*Mens* is the root of our word *mental*," Mrs. Parker continued.

Marina raised her hand. "Is that where the word *men* comes from?"

Boys again, Alice thought. She tried to catch Sarah's eye; but Sarah was not only sitting next to Hilary, she was whispering to her.

"That's a very interesting question, Marina," Mrs. Parker replied. "Actually the word *man* comes from the ancient Asian Sanskrit word *manu,* which means 'human being,' or 'man.'"

Mrs. Parker turned toward the blackboard. "You can see from the Latin expression that the Romans thought good health was good for your mind. And exercise was important for good health. So the Romans made athletics an important part of their educational system. They followed the earlier Greek ideal of a well-educated person as someone who excelled both intellectually and athletically." Mrs. Parker peered at the class over the top of her glasses. "Who remembers when the Olympic Games began? Do you know, Cynthia?"

"In 776 B.C., Mrs. Parker. The games were supposed to bring all the Greeks from different places together. So they would stop fighting."

"That's right. The Olympic Games began as a Greek festival, which was held every four years. The games were dedicated to Zeus, king of the gods, whose most important temple was located in Olympia." Mrs. Parker pulled down a map of Europe and pointed to Greece. "Olympia is right here, in the northwest. In order for the games to take place, all wars had to stop. The original Olympic Games were different from those we have today. They were more than athletic contests. Men also competed for prizes in music and literature."

"Weren't there any women contestants?" Alice asked.

"No, Alice. For the most part, Greek women stayed at home. They did the spinning and weaving and looked after the young children. The girls in Sparta were an exception. They were encouraged to practice athletics along with the boys. Since Sparta was a military state, every citizen was expected to defend it if necessary."

"Didn't the Spartans leave babies outside to die if they didn't look strong?" Jane asked.

"Yes, they did," Mrs. Parker replied.

"Pssst!" Lydia nudged Sarah. "Too bad some of the Turnips didn't get left out."

"What did you get if you won in the Olympics?" Hilary asked. "Did they have silver cups? Or gold medals, the way they do at horse shows?"

"No, Hilary," Mrs. Parker said. "The winners were crowned with a wreath of wild olive leaves and given a palm branch."

"Is that all? What about advertising contracts?" Sarah wanted to know. Her father used several famous athletes to advertise products.

"No. There was no advertising in ancient Greece. People made most things for themselves or bought them in small local shops. Advertising wasn't necessary the way it is today when we have so many products competing with one another. But the victors did win the right to erect a statue in the central enclosure of the sacred temple precinct. That was a great honor." Mrs. Parker looked at the clock. Class was almost over. "One more thing, girls," she said. "Don't forget to work on your cheers for the contest."

The bell rang. The girls hurried to their next class.

That day, Alice was late to lunch. The combination lock on her locker had jammed, and her lunch box was inside. It took a while for Mr. Avebury, the school superintendent, to open it.

By the time Alice arrived in the cafeteria, the Peaches were already seated at their favorite corner table. Caroline and Toni had joined the group. Alice went up to the table. No one said a word, and no one moved over. Alice felt terrible. She found an empty table and sat down. She saw herself eating lunch alone every day for the next seven years, until she graduated from Miss Barton's.

"Do you remember when James Bond was skiing in the Alps and the Russian assassins were chasing him?" Lydia asked later that day in gym class.

"What's that got to do with soccer?" Sarah was the captain of the Greens, and today was the first practice soccer game between the Greens and the Whites. Donna was captain of the Whites. The teams were huddled on opposite sides of the gym, discussing strategy.

"A lot," Lydia replied, "if you just listen. In order to get away from the assassins, James Bond zigzagged through the snow down the mountain. That made it harder for them to shoot him. He kept moving and he didn't go in a straight line, so they were never sure where he was."

"So?" Sarah sounded annoyed.

"So that's what *we* should do."

"Ski? In the snow? Down a mountain? Be serious, Lydia!" Hilary was at her most sarcastic.

"No, not ski, stupid. Dribble. Look, Sarah. You're center forward, right? So when you put the ball into play, you kick it to me. Since I'm the inside left forward, I'll be right next to you and all you have to do is tap it to me. Just so it goes over the center line and gets into play. The Whites won't expect such a little kick. Then I'll kick the ball backward to Wing Chu, who is inside right forward, opposite me. That will surprise them. Wing Chu and Hilary, the right wing, can kick the ball back and forth to each other as they zigzag down the right-hand side of the field. The Whites will be so confused that they won't know where the ball is going next. Just like the assassins after James Bond. Before Wing Chu and Hilary reach the goal, they kick the ball back over to me or Marina on the left. And we'll kick it in." Lydia finally paused for breath; a big satisfied smile lit up her face. Secret strategies always appealed to her.

"Well . . ." Sarah sat cross-legged with her elbows on her knees. Her chin rested in her cupped hands, and she was frowning in concentration. Her teammates sat in a circle around her. "What do the rest of you think?" Sarah asked them.

"It's worth a try," Marina said. "Especially since Nina and Jennifer are opposite Hilary and Wing Chu. Nina and Jennifer are the weakest players on the White team."

Marina wasn't the easiest person to get along with, Alice thought, but she was good at sizing up the opposition.

"All right, then, we'll try it." Sarah looked up. "Now remember, everyone. This is the first practice game. But every game counts, both for getting on the interschool team and for our total score against the Whites at the end of the year. So play as hard as you can. And good luck."

Miss Plimsoll blew her whistle. Both teams took their positions.

Alice had a terrible cramp in her right leg. It was definitely better to keep moving. Every time she sat down, it got worse. Sarah had picked Alice to play left halfback. It was clear to Alice that Sarah wanted her in a position where she could do the least damage to the team. But Alice was confident. Even with a cramp, the Greens and the Peaches would see a new Alice. An athletic Alice. She had had over a week to work on getting in shape.

The Whites won the toss. It was their turn to kick off. Miss Plimsoll placed the ball on the center line in the kickoff circle. Donna took three steps backward and then ran forward and kicked. The ball went over Lydia's head directly toward Alice.

The ball bounced right in front of her. Alice tried to block it, but it bounced sideways. She put up her hands to protect her face, and they touched the ball.

Miss Plimsoll blew her whistle to signal a foul.

Alice groaned. You couldn't touch the ball with your hands. That meant a penalty kick for the Whites, a mere eighteen feet from the goal!

Miss Plimsoll placed the ball on the penalty line.

Donna positioned herself for the kick. She drew back her right leg and kicked as hard as she could.

The ball sailed straight past Caroline, the Green goalie, and into the goal.

The Whites cheered. One minute into the game and the Whites were already ahead. All because of Alice Whipple. Not a single Green spoke to her.

Miss Plimsoll picked up the ball and returned to the center line. This time it was the Greens' turn to kick off. They agreed to try Lydia's James Bond strategy. Sarah gave the victory sign to the team, and Miss Plimsoll blew the whistle to start play.

Sarah tapped the ball to Lydia as she crossed the center line. Lydia kicked the ball backward, behind Sarah, to Wing Chu.

Alice watched as Hilary and Wing Chu deftly dribbled the ball back and forth between them, moving in a zigzag to avoid Nina and Jennifer. Cynthia and Jane, who played right halfback and center halfback for the Whites, fell back to protect their goal as Hilary and Wing Chu raced down the field. Kathy, right wing for the Whites, and Sandra, their left halfback, also ran over to block Hilary and Wing Chu. As a result, the members of both teams were bunched up on the other side of the gym, away from Alice. She was left completely alone on her side.

Alice wondered if she had done something wrong. Why was she all alone? Where was she supposed to be?

Alice watched in horror as Donna and Jane cut through the line of Greens protecting Wing Chu and Hilary. Donna got the ball away from them and kicked it over Hilary's head. The next thing Alice knew, the ball was sailing in the air over to her side of the gym. She ran forward as fast as she could toward the ball. Ten feet from the goal she lost her footing and felt herself propelled through the air. She heard a thud. Everything went black, and she saw stars. The next minute she was lying on her stomach on the gym floor, the breath knocked out of her. Her teammates helped her to her feet as they jumped up and down cheering.

"Alice, that was great!"

Alice detected a hint of respect in Sarah's voice.

"How did you think of that, Alice?" asked Wing Chu. "It was brilliant. The Whites never expected you to hit the ball into the goal with your head."

Alice didn't want to admit that she hadn't expected it either. Her head throbbed. But it was worth it. The Peaches were talking to her again. She hoped none of her teammates noticed her untied shoelace. If it hadn't been for that, she wouldn't have tripped, and if she hadn't tripped, she wouldn't have hit the ball with her head. Alice wondered how many other soccer goals were made by mistake. She didn't want to make goals by mistake. She wanted to be able to control the ball. Alice had tasted victory, and it definitely appealed to her. She was now more determined than ever.

The score was one-all. Before the end of the first half, the Greens were in the lead 4 to 1. Sarah, Hilary, and Lydia were in top form. Wing Chu was playing well, too. So was Marina.

But just before halftime, the tide turned. Donna and the

Whites got their second wind. Four goals in a row! Sarah decided that a pep talk was necessary in the seven minutes they were allowed for halftime. And a new strategy. The Greens huddled on their side of the gym.

"What about a slightly different version of the James Bond play?" Lydia suggested. "The Whites will think it's the same thing and be fooled. Here's how it goes: Sarah kicks the ball just over the line to Wing Chu, who sends the ball back to Toni at center halfback. Toni kicks it to Marina, who dribbles it to me, and we go down the field the way Hilary and Wing Chu did. If we get into trouble, we kick the ball back to Toni, and she and Marcia at right halfback take over."

"It's worth a try," Sarah said. "Somehow we have to stop their momentum."

Miss Plimsoll blew the whistle to resume play. For the next twenty minutes, nothing seemed to work for either team. The score stayed at 5 to 4 with the Whites one goal ahead. Neither team could break through. Finally Sandra, the White left halfback, used her hands to block Sarah, and Miss Plimsoll called a foul. Sarah had a penalty kick. She made a goal. The score was five-all with four minutes left in the game.

Alice was tired. She had run up and down the field at least twenty times. In fact, her lungs ached, her leg cramp still bothered her, and her head throbbed.She had made sure that her shoelaces were double-knotted, but she hadn't been involved in a single play since her dramatic goal. If people knew exactly how and why she had made the goal, they wouldn't be so impressed. Alice wished the game was over. Maybe soccer wasn't her thing.

Alice's thoughts were interrupted as Sarah kicked the ball into play. Lydia's modified James Bond strategy was finally beginning to work. Lydia kicked the ball to Toni, who sent it back to Marina. Lydia and Marina ran forward, dribbling the ball toward the White goal. But Donna suddenly cut in and reached the ball just before Marina was about to kick it. She sent the ball backward to Jane, who kicked it back to Donna. Donna had raced ahead nearly to Alice, dangerously near the Green goal.

Alice decided that this was her chance. She had to intercept the ball and kick it as far away from the goal as possible. She positioned herself in front of the goal to block Donna's kick. The ball came right toward her. *This is it,* Alice thought. *Here's my big chance.* She swung her right leg back and kicked forward. But she overdid it. The momentum was too much. Alice missed the ball entirely. It went through her legs and into the goal. Alice had kicked so hard that her feet flew out from beneath her. She landed flat on her bottom.

This time there was no cheering from the Greens or compliments from the Peaches.

Miss Plimsoll blew the whistle. The game was over. The Whites had won, 6 to 5. And all because Alice Whipple couldn't kick a soccer ball.

CHAPTER SIX

AN ALMOST-
PERFECT KICK

"**A**ha! I caught you!" Beatrice shouted at Alice, who was sitting at the kitchen table later that afternoon. Beatrice had crept into the kitchen, using the silent spy walk that Lydia had taught her when the Peaches were still friends with Alice. Alice was staring out the window, snacking on a bag of peanut M&M's. She hurriedly stuffed them into her uniform pocket. Alice didn't want to admit that she was upset at being excluded by the Peaches and that eating candy made her feel better.

"Everyone needs sugar for energy, especially athletes. When you swim long distances people in boats follow you and feed you chocolate."

"You're not an athlete and people don't swim in kitchens."

"Shut up, Beatrice. I'm thinking. I have something important to do. It requires energy and no distractions." Alice got up.

Before Beatrice had a chance to ask her where she was going, Alice slammed the front door and left the apartment.

"But it's *your* reputation I'm worried about, Peter," Alice said. She was sitting cross-legged on Peter's bed, telling him about the game. "Why would a world-famous soccer coach want his star pupil to fall down on the soccer field? There I was. Right in the middle of a crucial play. I missed a great chance to score a goal."

"I'm not a world-famous soccer coach, Alice. And you're definitely not a star pupil." Peter sat at his desk with his back to Alice. He didn't look up from his video game. He was playing "Super Mario Brothers Two."

"I'm your *only* pupil, Peter. There must be a reason for that. Good coaches have lots of pupils." Alice paused. "And I've only got four weeks left. So far I haven't seen any results from your coaching." Alice didn't mention her problems with the Peaches.

Peter didn't answer.

"Peter. You're not listening."

"I'm concentrating. Don't say another word. I'm almost at the end."

Alice fluffed up Peter's pillow and put it behind her back.

"There!" Peter declared. "That's the first time I rescued the princess."

"What a waste of time." Alice had never liked video games.

"Video games are good for eye-hand coordination," Peter said, "and eye-hand coordination is good for sports, especially ball games. Maybe you should ask your mother to get you some video games for your next birthday."

"I can't wait that long. I've got to improve *now.*"

"Then you're going to have to work harder. And that

means I have to work harder. And that means a lot of time. *My* time. I think I should get paid." Peter swiveled his desk chair around so that he was facing Alice.

"Paid? But *I* do all the work. All *you* do is sit and eat chocolate."

"That's not true. I have to organize your exercises, supervise you while you do them, check the stopwatch, monitor your progress, and make sure you don't goof off. And by the way, I hope you've been sticking to your diet. I hope you haven't been eating candy or ice cream."

Alice didn't mention the M&M's.

"You know," Peter said, "coaches are very well paid."

"Only the good ones."

"Alice, do you or don't you want a coach? Because I've been thinking of resigning."

That wouldn't do at all, Alice thought to herself. Without Peter, she would never make the team.

"Listen, Peter." Alice decided on a direct approach. "You're right. I really do have to improve in order to make the team. And you're the only person I know who's good enough to help me." Alice paused.

"Wel-l-l." Peter hesitated. He stared at Alice again.

"Please, Peter. This is really important."

"Look, Alice. That's what you said before. And then you ended up at Zorba's drinking a black cow. I don't believe you're serious."

"Yes I am, Peter."

"Well, if you're serious, you'll be willing to contribute to my allowance."

Alice sighed. "All right. How much?"

"If you gave me half your allowance, I might believe that you're really serious."

Alice agreed. Sometimes compromise was necessary, she realized.

"Okay, Alice," Peter said cheerfully. "We'll have to do a lot of working out. And we'll have to practice dribbling and kicking. But first I want you to try some new leg exercises." Peter stood up straight with his back against his bedroom wall. He slid down until he looked as if he were sitting in a chair, only there was no chair. His knees were bent so that his legs formed a right angle. "See this position? This is the way skiers strengthen their upper and lower legs. Now you try it."

Alice did.

"That's perfect. Stay like that while I go and get the equipment for the park. I'll be right back."

"Hurry up. This is very uncomfortable. I need a chair."

"That *proves* you're out of shape. It doesn't work with a chair. It only works without a chair. Remember, don't move." Peter left the room and shut the door behind him.

Peter and Alice walked down Fifth Avenue to the Metropolitan Museum of Art. Peter carried the soccer ball. His stopwatch and a large whistle hung from his neck. He wore his purple-and-white-striped soccer shirt with a big number 10 on the back. Alice thought he really did look like a soccer coach. She made up her mind to try as hard as she could. She took deep breaths and swung her arms around to loosen up. Her thighs hurt a bit.

When they reached the museum, they turned right and entered Central Park. Alice was feeling enthusiastic. As they walked to the playing field, she imagined herself making one fantastic kick. The ball would fly over the heads of the Courtney team, landing just in front of the goal. Sarah would gently tap it in and make the point. Alice's classmates would be jumping up and down. Sarah would give her the victory sign. They would be friends again.

"Maybe we should jog a little before we start kicking, Peter."

"Good idea, Alice." Peter was surprised by Alice's enthusiasm. "Four times around the field."

"Four?" Alice said doubtfully. "I'm still sore from the leg exercises and from playing soccer at school."

"That's nothing, Alice. If you run, the soreness will go away."

"It will?" Peter's logic escaped her.

"Yes. Because when you run, your body makes endorphins, natural painkillers. You'll see. Come on." Peter was off.

Alice followed.

On the second time around she couldn't help noticing that her breathing was much more regular than when she first began running. In fact, she was hardly puffing at all. Peter had told her that her lung capacity would increase. It obviously had. Alice was pleased with her progress. Perhaps one day she would even run in the marathon.

Alice's daydream of running in the marathon was interrupted by loud yapping. Out of the corner of her eye, she saw what looked like a large yellow fur ball roll up to her. Before she knew what had happened, the fur ball had turned into a Pekingese that was running wildly under her feet and nipping at her ankles. Alice began to run faster than she believed possible. She wasn't even sore. Peter had been right about the endorphins. She caught up to him in a flash.

"Let's get out of here," she gasped. "There's a huge dog after me!"

"What dog?" Peter slowed down and looked around. "You mean that little Pekingese over there?"

Alice turned.

The Pekingese was waddling demurely beside a little old lady. But that wasn't the worst of it. Not far from the Pekingese stood Muffie Singleton, Tiffany Painter, and Binky Loomis. They were bent over double, pointing and laughing at Alice.

"That dog's too fat and old to chase anyone," Peter said. Then he pointed toward the three girls. "Look at those girls over there, Alice. Do you know them? They seem to know you."

"They're those horrible Courtney girls." Alice was mortified. She knew that her father had been right about fat people being athletic. If fat people could be athletes, so could fat dogs. But the dog didn't look very threatening or athletic now. And it was embarrassing to have Muffie, of all people, see how scared she had been.

"Come on, Peter. Let's practice." Alice was glad to see the Courtney girls leave the park.

"Okay. What I want you to do first is practice dribbling." Peter dropped the ball on the ground and demonstrated how to dribble. He tapped the ball softly forward on a slight diagonal, first with one foot, then the other, as if the left foot were passing the ball to the right foot and back again. "Now you try it." Peter kicked the ball to Alice.

She blocked it with the side of her foot, exactly as Miss Plimsoll had shown her. She dribbled across the field as fast as she could. Peter yelled behind her.

Alice looked back and saw that he was waving his arms and blowing his whistle, signaling her to come back. She tried to turn the ball with her right foot, but instead of gently tapping it, she stepped on it. The next thing she knew, she was lying flat on the ground.

Peter rushed up to her.

"What do you think you're doing, Alice? Hasn't Miss Parasol, or whatever her name is, taught you anything?"

"Plimsoll. It was an accident." Alice looked up at Peter from the grass. "If you hadn't been screaming, I wouldn't have looked behind. And if I hadn't looked behind, I would have kept my eye on the ball. And if I had kept my eye on the ball, I wouldn't have stepped on it. And—"

"That's not what I'm talking about," Peter said, "I'm talking about dribbling. Hasn't anyone ever taught you how to dribble?"

"Well, I thought I was doing okay."

"You're wrong. In the first place, you don't dribble with your toes. In fact, you never use your toes in soccer. You use the inside of your foot. Now get up. This is important. You have to practice. Let me show you."

Peter took the ball and dribbled across the field again.

Alice saw what he meant. Using the side of his foot did seem to give him more control.

Peter dribbled back to Alice. "Now you try," he said.

Alice got up.

Ten minutes later she really felt that she had the hang of it, although it was hard to get used to kicking with the inside of her feet. She naturally wanted to kick with her toes, the way she kicked when fighting with Beatrice. But the more she practiced, the better she was at it.

After another ten minutes, Peter decided that Alice had dribbled enough for one day. "Now it's time for kicking. Remember, never use your toes. First of all, it hurts. Second, they get black and blue and your toenails fall out. And third, you don't have any control when you kick with your toes."

Peter pointed across the field. "You stand over there and watch me kick the ball to you."

Alice ran over to the opposite side of the field and waited. Sure enough, Peter landed a perfect kick, and the ball sailed in an arc across the field, bouncing right in front of Alice.

"Now it's your turn," Peter shouted through cupped hands.

Alice took three steps backward. She paused, inhaled deeply, rocked back and forth on her heels, and ran straight for the ball as fast as she could. She imagined how the kick would look in slow motion. She felt her right instep make contact with the ball. But instead of the perfect arc she expected, the ball rolled for a few feet and stopped.

Shaking his head, Peter ran up. "No, no," he said. "You hit too high up on the ball, Alice. A ball is a sphere. Think of the globe. If you hit it above the equator, you don't get any momentum. You've got to come at it from underneath, below the equator. Try again."

Peter placed the ball on the ground in front of Alice. She walked a few steps backward. After taking another deep breath, she ran for the ball. This time her connection was flawless. She watched the ball arc and sail through the air.

"Terrific!" yelled Peter, running after the ball.

Alice followed. She had actually kicked it clear across the field! It landed in a clump of trees.

Suddenly Peter turned around and ran right toward Alice. He hadn't even bothered to pick up the ball. He passed Alice at top speed and yelled, "Hornets!"

It didn't take Alice long to realize what Peter meant. Her beautiful kick had landed in a hornets' nest! And the hornets were not pleased. She watched them swarm around the ball looking for the intruder. They were a lot worse than the Pekingese. Alice turned and ran as fast as she could after Peter.

"What about the ball?" Alice gasped as she slumped on the steps of the museum beside Peter. "It's still back there."

"Never mind the ball. We'll get it as soon as the hornets go away. Oh, and Alice . . ."

"What?"

"That was a big improvement. Next time you play soccer and have to run down the field . . ."

"Yes?"

"Pretend that the hornets are after you."

CHAPTER SEVEN

EARLY MORNING AT THE WHIPPLES'

"Ish Ka-bi-bi-ly
Oten Boten . . ."

Beatrice moaned and rolled over in her bed. It was Sunday morning a week later. Beatrice briefly opened her eyes, and saw it was still dark. She pulled the covers over her head and dropped back to sleep. She dreamed of old women in pointed black hats and long black cloaks riding through the air on broomsticks.

"Bo-bo-ba
Deeten-Doten . . ."

The women in Beatrice's dream circled around a bonfire,

51

throwing toads, spiders, and worms into a huge black caldron that steamed and bubbled. Their long white hair streamed out behind them from beneath their hats as they rode faster and faster. Their grinning, toothless mouths gaped. They chanted a strange chant:

"Wa Dash
Boom . . ."

Beatrice leapt out of bed. For a moment she couldn't remember where she was. Then she heard more of the chant:

"Al-a-ka
Wal-a-ka
Wal-a-ka
Sock . . ."

Beatrice realized that it wasn't a dream after all. The sounds were coming from Alice's room, directly across the hall. Beatrice tiptoed out of her room and pressed her ear to Alice's door.

"Boom
Dee-ay
Yahoo!"

Beatrice ran as fast as she could down the hall. "Mommy, Daddy! Wake up! Alice has gone crazy. She's having a fit." Beatrice rushed into her parents' room and tugged at her father's pajama sleeve.

Mr. Whipple was snoring. It was five o'clock in the morning.

"Daddy, Mommy! Wake up! Something terrible is happening!"

"What is it, Beatrice?" Mr. Whipple asked groggily. His eyes were covered with a black sleep mask. He needed total darkness to be able to sleep.

"It's Alice. She's gone crazy. Come and see."

"Who's crazy?" Mr. Whipple pushed up the sleep mask and peered blearily at Beatrice.

"It's Alice," Beatrice repeated. "She's doing weird things. She woke me up. I thought it was witches in my dream, but it wasn't. It was Alice. She's casting spells." Beatrice hopped impatiently from one foot to the other. "I'm not kidding. She's probably turned into a witch or a werewolf or a vampire. You have to come see. It's really serious."

"What's serious?" Mrs. Whipple took the earplugs out of her ears. She wore them so she wouldn't hear Mr. Whipple snore.

"She says Alice is a witch," Mr. Whipple replied.

Mrs. Whipple got up and followed Beatrice out of the bedroom. Her ankle was much better, and she could walk without crutches. Mr. Whipple staggered behind.

When Beatrice reached the hall, she turned to her parents and pressed her finger against her lips. "Shhhh! Don't make a sound. Werewolves and vampires can hear everything." Beatrice tiptoed down the hall. Her parents followed. The noise got louder.

"Shish-ka-bobbily
Bagel-dagel
Yum yum
For Häagen-Dazs . . .

Mr. and Mrs. Whipple stared at each other.

"Kit Kat
Yay . . ."

Mr. Whipple carefully turned Alice's doorknob.

"Pea-nut bars and
Choc-olate Chips,
Ched-dar Cheese and
Rice . . ."

Mr. Whipple gingerly pushed open the door.

"Gum,
Pâ-té, and
Mars Bars, too . . ."

Alice stopped. She had lost her concentration. Out of the corner of her eye, she saw three astonished faces reflected in the full-length mirror on her wall. She whirled around. "Daddy! Mommy! Beatrice! What are you doing here?"

"What are *you* doing, young lady?" Mr. Whipple demanded. He opened the door all the way. "Do you realize that it's five o'clock in the morning? You scared Beatrice."

Beatrice beamed. "Check her teeth, Daddy," she said. "If she's a werewolf, she'll have fangs."

"Quiet, Beatrice," Mrs. Whipple ordered.

"And claws too," Beatrice went on. "Check for claws. And fur. Werewolves get covered with fur."

"Mary." Mr. Whipple turned to his wife. "How many times

have I told you that you shouldn't let her see horror movies on TV?"

"She doesn't let me see them," Beatrice said. "I watch them at James's and Peter's."

"Well, you shouldn't see them there either." Mr. Whipple turned to Alice. "What exactly *are* you doing, Alice? Isn't it awfully early for you to be up?"

"I'm practicing cheers, Daddy. You know, for the inter-school soccer game with Courtney. We're having a cheer-writing contest. And I'm making up new words for old cheers."

"About food?"

"You burn up a lot of calories playing soccer, Daddy," Alice pointed out. "And you get really hungry."

"All right, Alice." Her father sighed. "Now please go back to bed so that the rest of us can get some sleep." Mr. and Mrs. Whipple sent Beatrice back to her room, switched off the hall light, and went to bed themselves.

About an hour later, Mr. and Mrs. Whipple were awakened by a persistent, rhythmic beat. Their bedroom floor shook slightly. Mr. Whipple pushed up his sleep mask for the second time that morning and swung his feet out of bed into his slippers. "It's all right, Mary," he said. "I'll see what it is this time." Mr. Whipple opened the bedroom door and listened. The noise was coming from the study.

The study door was open. Alice had turned on the television set. She was dressed in a green bathing suit with pink and white polka dots and a pair of orange tights. A morning exercise program on low-impact aerobics blared forth. "Now, girls," lisped the slim young man leading three rows of women in brightly colored leotards, "let's do a few stretches to limber up and get our blood circulating." He lifted his arms above his head as if he were reaching for the ceiling.

Alice did the same. She watched as the man and the women bent their knees slightly and touched their toes the way Peter had taught her.

"Okay, ladies. Now that we're warmed up, let's start our routine."

As the class stepped to the left, Alice bumped into the bookshelf on the right. As the class moved to the right, Alice knocked the telephone off its stand.

It looks easy when he does it, Alice thought.

When the class marched forward, Alice marched backward—and bumped right into her father.

"Alice!" Mr. Whipple was leaning against the doorframe, his arms folded across his chest.

Alice turned around. She could see how angry he was, and she had to think quickly. "You should do some exercises, Daddy," she said. "If you did more exercise, you would sleep better. You'd probably stop waking up. Exercise helps relax your muscles."

"Alice, do you realize that it is six o'clock in the morning and the television is much too loud? Please turn it off. And return to your room and be very, very quiet for at least the next hour and a half. You might even try reading a book." Mr. Whipple didn't wait for a reply. He stumbled back to bed.

Finally Mr. Whipple gave up. It was impossible to get back to sleep. He got out of bed and dressed quietly to avoid waking his wife. He was hungry and decided that a good breakfast was what he needed. Bacon and eggs, he thought. And toast with jam. Orange juice and coffee. It sounded very comforting.

He made his way to the kitchen. Beatrice was already seated at the kitchen table watching Alice prepare her high-protein breakfast in the blender: one raw egg, two teaspoons of yeast, half a cup of lowfat yogurt, a tablespoon of wheat germ, two tablespoons of honey, and a quarter cup of sunflower seeds.

Alice pushed the liquefy button.

"What is red and green and whirls around?" Beatrice asked.

"Quiet, Beatrice. I'm concentrating."

"A frog in a blender, stupid."

Mr. Whipple decided to skip breakfast.

CHAPTER EIGHT
PETER AND THE TURNIPS

For the next week, Peter worked with Alice almost every day after school. She jogged, jumped rope, and practiced dribbling. On Saturday morning Peter called her.

"I have an idea, Alice," he said. "You've been doing so well that I think you're ready for something new."

"You do?" Alice wished the Peaches were as pleased with her progress as Peter was. But they were still ignoring her. Even though Peter was helping her a lot, she still wasn't doing well in the practice games.

"Yes. Swimming. It's a very good aerobic exercise, which will improve your general fitness, not just your legs."

"Where are we going to swim?"

"At the Y. My parents have a family membership, and they're taking us with them. They said I could invite you and Beatrice to come, too. Do you have a bathing suit?"

"Of course I have a bathing suit." Alice didn't mention that she was actually *wearing* her bathing suit, which she put on to do her early television exercises.

"Good. You'll need a bathing cap too. And a towel. Tell Beatrice. Meet us out front in an hour."

"You said swimming, Peter." Alice was pedaling as fast as she could on the stationary bicycle in the large exercise room at the Y.

Mr. and Mrs. Hildreth were showing Beatrice and James how to use the exercise machines as Alice struggled under Peter's watchful eye.

"We'll get to that, Alice. First things first. This is warm-up. Besides, bike riding is also aerobic." Peter peered at the meter, which clocked Alice's speed and the average number of calories burned up per hour. "I think you're a bit slow," he said. "You're only going ten miles an hour."

Alice speeded up.

"That's better. Keep it up for ten minutes. Watch the needle on the meter and make sure it stays on fifteen. It's only eleven o'clock anyway; the pool isn't open for kids under eighteen for another hour."

"Hey! Look at me," Beatrice called out from across the room. She was running but she wasn't getting anywhere. "It says I've gone up four flights of stairs."

"Oh, shut up," Alice said, puffing.

"We'll do that one next," Peter said.

"What do you mean *we*? You're not doing anything," Alice said between gulps of air.

"Stop talking, Alice. Talking interferes with your breathing."

"Look at *me*," James said from the rowing machine. "I've already rowed one mile."

"We'll do that one after the stairs," Peter said. "Rowing is very good for your upper torso, especially your pectoral and trapezius muscles."

Alice didn't answer. She decided to save her breath.

Two miles of rowing and three flights of stairs later, it was noon; time for the pool to open. Alice, Peter, James, and Beatrice accompanied the Hildreths to the locker room.

Five minutes later, Peter was settled in one of the deck chairs by the side of the Olympic-size pool. He held his stopwatch.

James and Beatrice dove in. "Let's play Marco Polo," James said.

"Aren't you going swimming, Peter?" Alice asked.

"Maybe later. I've got to concentrate on timing you. Are you ready for some laps?"

Alice stood by the edge of the pool. It seemed like a long way to the other end.

"I think you should start with the sidestroke to limber up," Peter said. "Do two laps first, and then we'll see about the rest."

Alice put her feet right on the edge of the pool and curled her toes around the rim. She dove in and began swimming. "Hey!" she called out. "Beatrice and James are in my way." They were at the shallow end in the middle of a serious game of Marco Polo, a combination of water tag and blindman's buff. "And they're making waves."

"Swim around them. Waves are good practice," Peter said.

Alice had completed her second lap of the sidestroke. She clung to the edge of the pool to catch her breath. Just then she saw Donna and Jane emerge from the locker room. Both girls were in suits and caps, ready to swim. Following behind them were no less than *four* Turnips: Sandra, Ellen, Cynthia, and

Tracey. In fact, the very same Turnips who made up Lydia's list of likely choices for the interschool soccer team. They had all come to swim. Tracey's mother was with them.

"Hi, Alice. What are you doing here?" Donna asked as she approached the pool. "I didn't know you could swim."

Alice detected a distinct sneer in Donna's voice.

Donna did a perfect racing dive and swam at top speed back and forth across the pool.

Alice saw Peter sit up and take note.

Then Jane and the rest of the Turnips dove in.

Alice climbed out of the pool and sat down next to Peter. "It's too crowded for my laps," she complained.

"Who're those girls, Alice? They sure can swim."

"Those are Turnips. They wouldn't interest you."

Peter knew about the Peaches and Turnips, but he could never see any significant differences between them.

"Look at the way that girl does the crawl." Peter pointed to Donna. "Each stroke is nice and smooth. And she breathes regularly. You go back in and do five laps of the crawl."

Peter stood up to watch Donna. Alice heard Cynthia and Ellen whispering about how cute he was. "I love freckles," Cynthia said. "Nice smile," Ellen added. Not only were Cynthia and Ellen fast runners and good swimmers, Alice realized, but they were short, just like Peter. Tracey and Sandra weren't very tall either, as Alice thought about it. Even Donna was shorter than Peter. In fact, Jane was the only tall Turnip. Alice decided that she would have to keep an eye on them or else Peter would get distracted.

"Okay, Alice. In you go." Peter checked the stopwatch.

Alice jumped in as the Turnips climbed out of the pool.

As Alice did the crawl, she noticed that she had a new problem. Peter wasn't paying as much attention as usual to his stopwatch. In fact, he wasn't even looking at it anymore. He was surrounded by Turnips and clearly enjoying every minute of it. To make matters worse, Tracey's mother was deep in conversation with Mr. and Mrs. Hildreth.

When Alice overheard snatches of Peter's conversation with the Turnips, she was really concerned. It was hard to make out exactly what was being said because of all the splashing and shouting, which echoed through the room. But she did hear Donna ask Peter what his favorite activity was. When Peter replied that it was drama, Donna told him about the ninth grade interschool production of *Gulliver's Travels* and suggested that he might like to see it. "All of us are in it." Tracey smiled proudly. "We're the Lilliputians, the little people who tie up Gulliver when he lands on their island. It's lucky they needed short people, so we get to be in the play."

Uh-oh, thought Alice. *I've got to do something. Peter is getting too interested in the Turnips.* "Oh, Peter!" she shouted from across the pool.

"Five more laps, Alice," he shouted back.

Alice had no choice but to swim. *Should I pretend to drown?* she wondered. But she dismissed the idea as too embarrassing in front of six Turnips. She would never live it down. *I could slip on the steps and sprain my ankle,* she thought. *But then I wouldn't make the soccer team. If only James or Beatrice would start drowning so Peter would have to jump in and save them.* But they were being good for once and staying in the shallow end.

Alice swam over to Peter's side of the pool and hoisted herself out. "Okay, Peter," she said. "That's it for today. We should be getting home. Beatrice has been in the water long enough."

"I have not," Beatrice declared. "I heard what you said,

Alice. Just because you're too lazy to swim doesn't mean *I* have to go."

"Oh shut up, Beatrice. Your hair is going to turn green from the chlorine and your eyes are already red."

"They are not!"

"Why don't you rest for a few minutes, Alice?" Peter suggested.

"Peter is right," Donna said. "We're having a good time. We don't want Peter to go yet." She and the other Turnips turned their backs on Alice and continued their conversation with Peter.

Alice sighed. "All right." She realized that Peter had no intention of leaving as long as the Turnips were still there. And if Peter stayed, Alice would stay. She spread out her towel and sat down on the chair next to Peter's so she could hear what was being said. She closed her eyes and pretended to be dozing.

Jane checked the clock on the wall behind the lifeguard stand. "It's time for lunch," she said. "My mother's expecting us back soon." The Turnips were all having lunch at Jane's house.

"Maybe Peter would like to come," Donna suggested. "We're going to practice soccer after lunch."

Alice opened her eyes and looked at Peter. "We still have some things to do, Peter."

"We can do them later," Peter replied. "I'm going to Jane's for lunch."

"Peter, you should be ashamed of yourself," Alice fumed over the telephone. "You're being paid to be my coach. Coaches don't desert their players in the middle of a practice session."

"You could have done more laps."

"That's not the point. We made an agreement, and time is running out." Alice paused. Peter said nothing. "I hope you enjoyed your lunch," Alice continued. "I didn't know you were so girl crazy."

"I am *not* girl crazy!"

"Listen, Peter. I know you said you didn't want to see the interschool soccer match. But if you keep on being my coach and don't get completely distracted by girls, you can come to the match, and you'll be able to meet *tons* of girls."

"Wel-l-l," Peter said slowly.

Alice breathed a sigh of relief. She had to admit that sometimes the Turnips had their good points.

CHAPTER NINE

REALIGNMENT

On Monday Donna was waiting for Alice at the end of the lunch line. Alice's tray was empty except for her lunch box and a small container of skim milk.

"Hi, Alice," Donna said. She had a large plate of spaghetti and meatballs on her tray. "I think your friend, Peter Hildreth, is very nice."

"Yes, he is. We've been friends for years. He lives right across the street from me." Alice still hadn't completely forgiven Peter for deserting her at the Y. And she thought it was typical of the Turnips to encourage him.

"How often do you see him?"

"Almost every day. He's been helping me practice to get on the soccer team."

"That's why you've gotten so much better at gym. He must be a really good coach." Alice was amazed; Donna actually sounded friendly.

If Donna could appreciate her improvement, Alice

thought, then what was wrong with the Peaches? "He *is* a good coach," Alice replied. "He's captain of his class soccer team. In fact," Alice continued, thinking fast, "I could probably arrange for Peter to help you practice after school."

"*Could* you, Alice?"

Alice couldn't believe it. What might have been a total disaster was turning into a very promising situation. Not only did she see a way to keep Peter as her coach, but Donna could be a great help too. Everyone knew that Miss Plimsoll would pick Donna to be the captain of the interschool soccer team. Since Alice had every intention of making the team, it would help if Donna liked her. Then maybe Donna would give her a good position.

"Of course, if Peter coaches you, I'd have to be there, too. I'm sure that if I ask him, Peter will agree. We have three afternoons left before Miss Plimsoll picks the team."

"Why don't you come and sit with us, Alice?" Donna said. "We can talk about it and arrange where to meet."

Alice and Donna carried their trays through the lunch room, past the Peaches' favorite corner table, where Lydia, Hilary, and Marina were sitting. Alice followed Donna to the Turnips' table and sat next to her. The three Peaches stared at Alice. She had to bite her lip to keep from grinning.

CHAPTER TEN

PEANUTS AND MARSHMALLOWS

Alice was growing tired of her liquid diet breakfast. It did not taste very good, and by the time she got to science class, she was always starving. Thursday morning was no exception.

As she passed Mr. Moffet's desk, Alice couldn't help noticing a small can of Planter's peanuts and a package of miniature marshmallows on the windowsill. They were right next to his coffee machine. The peanut can was open and only half full. Perhaps Mr. Moffet wouldn't notice if she had just one, she thought.

By the time the rest of the class arrived, the can was empty and there were only four marshmallows left.

Alice sat down and Donna sat next to her.

"Well, girls"—Mr. Moffet strode back and forth in front of the class as he talked—"this is the last day of our nutrition unit. I have an experiment planned for today that will demon-strate how we measure the calorie content of food." The thick rubber soles on his brown suede shoes squeaked against the linoleum floor. He was tall and unusually thin; he wore a gold earring in his left ear and played the bass in a jazz band on weekends. Even though the girls at Miss Barton's thought he was weird, everyone agreed that he was a great teacher.

"Before we begin the experiment, I'll hand back your homework on food groups and your calorie charts."

Each fifth-grader had given him a record of the food and calories she had consumed over a one-week period.

"Judging from your reports," Mr. Moffet continued, "I would say that hamburgers are the staple in the fifth-grade diet. Do you all know what a staple is?"

Wing Chu raised her hand. "It's the main thing that people eat. Like rice in China."

"The English eat rice pudding," Hilary added.

"Rice is not an English staple, Hilary," Mr. Moffet said. He wrote *staple* on the board. "A staple is usually produced in the country where it is eaten, and the English do not produce rice."

"But when I'm in England, I eat a lot of rice pudding. It must be a staple."

Alice happened to know that Hilary had only been to En-gland twice in her life. "My father went to a business dinner in England," Alice said. "He had *two* kinds of potatoes in the same meal."

"That's right, Alice. Potatoes are the English staple. Every country has a staple food, except perhaps America because there are so many different nationalities here. Rice is the Chi-nese staple, pasta in Italy, corn for tortillas in Mexico, and so on." Mr. Moffet handed back the papers.

"Most of you seem fairly consistent in the number of calories you ate. Except, that is, for Alice." He turned to her. "Your lists are completely different. For example, on the first day you ate three thousand six hundred and forty-five calories, which is many more than you need, and on the second day, you ate eight hundred and fifteen, which is not nearly enough. Why is that?"

"She went on a diet," Marina said, giggling. "Boys don't like fat girls," she added under her breath so Mr. Moffet wouldn't hear.

Alice pretended not to have heard Marina. "Actually, Mr. Moffet, I left out breakfast on the second day." She decided to ignore the subject of dieting. "It was because of the frog in the blender."

"The frog in the blender?" Mr. Moffet raised his eyebrows; they made two brown arches.

"Ugh!" Cynthia made a face. "Did you turn on the blender with the frog in it?"

"What I mean is," Alice explained, "I skipped breakfast that day."

"It's not a good idea to skip breakfast, Alice."

"No, Mr. Moffet."

"Good. Now let us discuss just what a calorie is." Mr. Moffet peered at the class. "Do you know, Marina?"

"It's what makes you fat." Marina grinned at Alice.

"You gain weight by eating more calories than you burn up because the body stores extra food energy as fat," Mr. Moffet explained. "But you need calories; they keep you alive and active. Donna, can you define *calorie*?"

"A calorie is a measure of the heat energy value of food." Donna always knew the answer.

"Excellent, Donna." Mr. Moffet looked at the class. "How do calories affect our bodies?"

Sarah raised her hand. "Calories give us the energy we need to do things."

"That's right, Sarah." Mr. Moffet paused. "The exact definition of a calorie is the amount of heat necessary to raise the temperature of a thousand grams of water one degree Celsius. And now for our experiment. Since we measure the calorie content of foods in terms of the heat they produce, we'll burn two kinds of food and measure how high they raise the temperature of water. Whichever makes the water hotter has the most calories. We're going to do the experiment in teams of two and we'll compare a peanut with a miniature marshmallow."

"Uh-oh," Alice muttered to herself.

That afternoon in gym class Donna kicked the ball between Wing Chu and Sarah. Toni tried to block it, but Jane was too quick for her. Jane intercepted the ball and dribbled it toward the goal. Caroline, the Green goalie, was too far to the right. It looked as if Jane had a clear shot to the goal. But Alice, who was playing left fullback, cut across the goal and blocked Jane's kick.

Miss Plimsoll blew the whistle.

Alice was glad she had eaten the peanuts and marshmallows, even if Mr. Moffet's experiment had been ruined. She was sure the extra calories had given her the energy she needed to make an effective last-minute play.

Gym was only half over, but Miss Plimsoll wanted to use the remaining time to announce her choices for the interschool soccer match and to select the two best cheers.

The girls sat on the gym floor as Miss Plimsoll read off the list of names in alphabetical order. Alice held her breath. It was a long way from the *A*'s to the *W*'s. Alice thought about her efforts to shape up. She had had a difficult five weeks of training: 398 laps around the block; 273 laps back and forth across the huge pool at the Y; 22 half hours of jumping rope; 148 miles on the rowing machine; 103 flights on the stair machine; and 93 miles uphill on the exercise bicycle at 10 miles an hour. And three afternoon practice sessions with the Turnips. All that and only one black cow, and a pack of peanut M&M's. *And* one *small* half can of Mr. Moffet's peanuts and a few miniature marshmallows, which had actually been a help, even though they were rather stale. Alice had not lost much weight; but her thighs no longer wobbled and she had more stamina than before. The big question was, would it all pay off? Would she make the team and show the Peaches?

Miss Plimsoll reached the *T*'s. It would not be long now. Alice had to admit she was nervous. Her status as a Peach was at stake. Even though Alice had been spending time with the Turnips, her loyalty was still to the Peaches. So far five Peaches and five Turnips had been chosen.

Alice's heart sank. Miss Plimsoll announced the last name, which began with a *V.* It was Ellen Vanderlyn, a Turnip.

Donna and Jane congratulated each other.

Lydia groaned. There were six Turnips and only five Peaches on the team.

All Alice's work had been for nothing. The Peaches would never speak to her again. Even Peter would forget all about her. He would spend all his time with Donna. And Donna wouldn't need her anymore.

Alice was so disappointed that she didn't hear Miss Plimsoll announcing the three substitutes until her own name was called.

Alice perked up. There was a glimmer of hope. Although she was not on the team, there was a lot to be said for being a substitute. First of all, in soccer the substitutes got to play often. Second, the substitute was always fresher and more rested than the other players. Third, and most important, the substitute introduced a new element into the game, a dramatic element. Like making a grand entrance onstage. If she could make a grand entrance *and* score a spectacular goal . . . Suddenly she felt much better!

She was quite confident as Miss Plimsoll turned to the subject of the cheers. Alice always got good grades on creative writing assignments. The year before, she had won the lower school poetry contest. Only six fifth graders had written cheers, and Alice knew that she was the best writer in the class. The girls would vote for two cheers.

"Would the Whites read their cheers first?" Miss Plimsoll said.

Donna stood up. "One, three, five, nine," she recited. "Who do we think is mighty fine? Courtney, Courtney, yay!"

Ellen stood up. "Two, four, six, eight. Courtney girls are really great! Yay, Courtney!"

Jane was last. "Twenty, thirty, forty, fifty. Who do we think is really nifty? Courtney, Courtney, yay!"

Really, thought Alice. *How unoriginal.*

"Very good, Whites. Now the Greens."

Lydia began. "C-I-A. M-I-5. K-G-B. Courtney, Courtney, is the team for me."

Alice didn't think Miss Plimsoll would choose Lydia's cheer.

Hilary went next. "I had a little horse. He went out for a trot. But he galloped for the Courtney team. Because they hit the spot."

Typical, Alice thought. She could tell Miss Plimsoll liked that one.

Finally Alice stood up. "Shish-ka-bobbily. Bagel-dagel. Yum yum, for Häagen-Dazs . . ."

Marina giggled.

Alice continued. She was glad that Marina appreciated the humor of her cheer.

"Kit Kat, yay!" Alice jumped and waved her arms over her head.

Hilary made a face at Lydia.

"Peanut bars and chocolate chips, cheddar cheese and . . ."

The effect was not as Alice had intended. The whole class was laughing at Alice instead of her cheer.

Alice quickly finished and sat down. The whole day had been a disaster. Even being a substitute couldn't make up for her embarrassment.

The class chose Hilary's cheer for the beginning of the match and Jane's for the end.

CHAPTER ELEVEN

THE BIG GAME

The afternoon of the soccer match, the Brophy Center was filled with fifth-grade parents, friends, teachers, and all the middle school classes of Miss Barton's and Courtney. The Whipples and Beatrice were sitting with the Hildreths. They had excellent seats, right over the center line. Peter and James were there too.

"Oh boy!" James let out a soft whistle. "This is a great soccer field. There must be millions of people here."

"It's all right." Peter was unimpressed. "I like outdoor games better."

"Look over there, Peter. The teams are coming." James pointed to both ends of the field. "There are the girls from the Y, Peter. The ones you met swimming."

Peter surveyed the soccer field. Sure enough, the six Turnips from the Y entered.

Peter was looking forward to getting to know Donna better.

"Look, Peter!" James jabbed his brother in the arm. "I can

see Alice! Her shirt has a number twelve on it and there are only eleven on a team."

"That's because she's a substitute," Peter explained.

Alice entered the field along with Miss Plimsoll, the eleven regular members of the team, and the two other substitutes. She had to admit that even though she was only a substitute and had lost the cheer contest, being in the midst of the action was a thrilling experience. She felt very professional in her soccer shirt and Miss Barton's blue shorts. *This must be the way the contestants felt in the Olympic Games,* she thought, *when they first entered the stadium.* She saw herself being crowned with a wreath of olive leaves. One of the judges handed her a palm branch and a flaming torch of victory.

Alice looked around at the crowd. She spotted her parents and the Hildreths and waved.

Alice watched the Courtney team enter the field. In contrast to the blue shorts and blue soccer shirts worn by the Miss Barton's team, the Courtney girls were in light green shorts and yellow shirts. All the shirts had large numbers on the back.

Miss Plimsoll and Mr. Whitney, the Courtney fifth grade gym and dance teacher, stood in the middle of the field. Mr. Whitney had short brown hair and a lot of freckles. He wore khaki pants and a light blue shirt. Both teachers had whistles hanging around their necks. Miss Plimsoll carried the soccer ball.

The players and the substitutes assembled in front of their goals for a last-minute pep talk by the team captains. Donna was the Miss Barton's captain and Muffie Singleton was the Courtney captain. Donna reviewed the signals for the strategies that they had been practicing for the match. "I'm counting on each and every one of you," Donna declared enthusiastically. "Remember that we're a team, and teams work together. We are going to beat Courtney and get that silver trophy back for Miss Barton's." Donna took a deep breath. "Now let's go out there and win!"

The audience grew quiet. Alice could feel the excitement. The Courtney team lined up in single file. Each girl placed her hands on the shoulders of the girl in front of her and shouted out a cheer to the tune of the "Bunny Hop." They bunny hopped around the field in an S curve and ended up back at center field. The audience applauded vigorously. Then Miss Barton's team lined up in order of height with Marina first and did Hilary's cheer, the first two lines while trotting in a straight line and the last two at a gallop. The audience clapped again.

"Do girls always act like that before a soccer game?" James whispered to Peter, who was staring at Donna. "It's stupid."

"Alice says it's a tradition," Peter replied, not taking his eyes off Donna.

Miss Plimsoll and Mr. Whitney blew their whistles and the teams took their positions on the field. Alice, Toni, and Caroline, Miss Barton's three substitutes, sat on the sideline benches to watch and wait.

Alice was pleased that the front line of Miss Barton's team was entirely composed of Peaches, even though they had done nothing to help her get on the team. Sarah was center forward, Lydia and Marina were on her left, and Wing Chu and Hilary on her right. Donna was center halfback. Ellen was left halfback and Cynthia was right halfback. The fullbacks were Sandra and Tracey, and Jane was goalie. Even if there were six Turnips and only five Peaches on the team, Alice thought, all three substitutes were Peaches, so if you counted the substitutes, there were actually more Peaches than Turnips. Alice definitely counted the substitutes.

The opposition, Alice also realized, was formidable. The front line included none other than Muffie Singleton, Tiffany Painter, and Binky Loomis. They certainly looked smug, Alice thought. It would be great to teach them a lesson. Then they would be sorry that they had laughed at her. Even better, they would lose the silver cup.

Alice waited anxiously on the sidelines all through the first half of the match. None of the substitutes for either team had been called. The game was so close that the captains were afraid to rock the boat. Courtney made the first goal on a penalty kick by Binky Loomis, and Miss Barton's made the second with a solid direct kick by Sarah. Courtney then made three goals with a strategy that Miss Barton's had not anticipated. Muffie Singleton, their center forward, kept sending the ball to the wings, who dribbled down the field and tapped it back to her at the last minute. Normally the center forward would try to score, but Muffie sent it back to the wing, who then kicked it past Jane into the goal. Finally Sandra and Tracey got wise to the strategy and blocked Muffie before she could pass the ball. Then Miss Barton's made three goals by following variations on Lydia's zigzagging James Bond ploy.

Halftime came and went. Alice was beginning to get hungry and bored. The score was 6 to 6, and Alice still hadn't played. She imagined herself scoring goal after goal, leading her team to victory. She tapped her foot to the rhythm of her cheer. "Shish-ka-bobbily. Bagel-dagel . . ." Alice hummed to herself. She began to fear the worst. Was it possible that all her work shaping up had been for nothing? Would her only reward be that Peter got to be friends with Donna and the other Turnips and lost interest in her? Had her parents and Beatrice wasted their whole Friday afternoon to watch Alice sit on a bench on the sidelines?

Alice noticed that the Courtney team was particularly good at dribbling the ball past the halfback by sticking close to one another and preventing the opposing players from getting to the ball. If only she could communicate her observations to Donna, maybe Miss Barton's would change their strategy in time to win.

All of a sudden, Muffie found an opening in Miss Barton's defense because Donna had moved too far toward Ellen. With a well-placed kick, made by the side of her foot just below the equator of the ball, Muffie sent the ball straight toward Miss Barton's goal. Jane lunged forward and blocked it.

A gasp went up from the crowd. Jane tripped and one of her legs seemed to fold up under her. The next thing Alice knew, Miss Plimsoll and Mr. Whitney were helping Jane, who was limping off the field.

Donna rushed over to the substitutes' bench and Alice saw her chance. "Listen, Donna," she said quickly, "you've got to watch the space between you and Cynthia. When you move left toward Ellen, then Muffie and Binky can rush into the open space with the ball. Then it's the two of them against Sandra, and they can easily kick the ball past her into the goal. They've done it three times."

Alice could see that Donna was impressed. "You're right, Alice," she said. "I'm going to send you in to take Jane's place. Keep an eye on Binky and Muffie in case they try it again."

"I certainly will." She hoped they would.

Alice stood in the goal. It was very different from being on the sidelines. She could feel the crowd in the stands on either side of the playing field. Alice was aware of Peter and her parents watching her. She bent over and touched her toes a few times to stretch her leg muscles and waved her arms around to loosen them up.

The score was still 6 to 6. Alice wished that there were more than twelve minutes left in the game. She was glad that she was finally on the field so that she could demonstrate her new athletic ability. But how was she going to lead her team and her school to victory? Goalies didn't make goals.

The whistle blew. Alice kept her eye on the ball as Sarah's first kick sent it across the field on a diagonal. Wing Chu was the first to reach it. Tiffany Painter shoved Wing Chu out of the way, allowing Binky Loomis to intercept the ball. Wing Chu crashed into Muffie and fell to the ground. She skinned her knee and limped off the field as the referee stopped play. Donna signaled to Caroline, who replaced Wing Chu.

Alice couldn't believe that the referee didn't call a foul against Tiffany.

After the ball was back in play, Binky dribbled it to the center halfback. She maneuvered the ball forward over the center line, past Lydia and Ellen. The only thing between the ball and a certain goal was Alice Whipple.

Alice saw the ball fly right toward her. She bent her head slightly and thrust her shoulders forward. The ball landed in front of her and she grabbed it. Before she could decide where to throw it, Muffie loomed up in front of her. Muffie was even taller than Marina. She leapt up and down, grimacing and waving her hands to make Alice fumble. No one saw that Muffie actually touched the ball and knocked it out of Alice's hands.

Another foul that had not been called! Alice was furious. Courtney girls were not only snobby and rude, they cheated as well.

Alice was so angry that she dove for the ball and grabbed it before Muffie could react. From a sitting position inside the goalie's area, Alice raised the ball over her head and threw it as hard as she could toward Sarah, taking the Courtney team completely by surprise.

Sarah passed to Hilary, the right wing. Hilary and Caroline dribbled the ball back and forth between them as they ran to the center line.

The Courtney center halfback intercepted the ball and kicked it back toward Muffie, who maneuvered it between Sandra and Tracey. Muffie kicked the ball straight toward Alice.

This time Alice was really ready for it. She blocked it and prepared to kick. Alice turned her foot sideways, remembered to kick below the equator of the ball, drew her right leg back, and kicked as hard as she could. She made perfect contact with the ball. It sailed over the heads of the onrushing Courtney team toward the center of the field.

And then Alice did a very unusual thing. With only thirty seconds left in the game and before Courtney had a chance to turn around and chase the ball, Alice left her post at the goal and raced forward. Her kick had landed the ball in front of Hilary, who was just over the center line. Hilary kept control of the ball as Alice zigzagged past Courtney *and* her own teammates until she was clear of them.

"Over here, Hilary!" Alice yelled. Hilary kicked the ball to Alice. Donna and Sarah raced to either side of Alice to protect her from being intercepted. The Courtney fullbacks were out of place. They had run forward, thinking that Courtney had a sure goal. Alice began her final kick with her right foot. Suddenly she shifted her weight and swiftly kicked the ball with her left instep. The ball whipped past the astonished Courtney goalie as the whistle blew.

The game was over. The score was 7 to 6. Miss Barton's had regained the silver cup and Alice was a heroine.

Alice, Hilary, Lydia, and Sarah were at their favorite corner table in the school cafeteria on Monday.

"We can blindfold them and make them wash their hands in a bowl of spaghetti," Hilary said.

"And we can borrow the skeleton from the science room and rattle its bones," Lydia added with a ghoulish expression on her face.

"I can use my tape recorder for weird sound effects: owls, bats, screams, rattling chains . . ." Hilary suggested.

Alice sipped her chocolate milk shake. "We could touch them with wet rubber gloves as they crawl through the dark tunnel."

"That's a great idea, Alice," Sarah said. "We could use paint that glows in the dark and line the tunnel wall with horrible faces."

The Peaches were making plans for the school fair. The fifth grade was in charge of the House of Horrors and Alice had been elected president of the planning committee. She thought it might be a good idea if a few Turnips were on the committee as well.

"Have some Brie, Alice." Hilary handed her a cracker with a generous slab of cheese on it.

"Thanks, Hilary." Alice took a bite. A little cheese wasn't so bad, she thought to herself, as long as you exercised.

Alice was relieved that things were finally back to normal.

ABOUT THE AUTHORS

LAURIE ADAMS is the coauthor of four other books featuring Alice Whipple. In addition, she has written three books on art as well as articles on art history and psychology. She is a professor of art history at the City University of New York and a psychoanalyst in private practice. She lives with her husband and their two children in New York City.

ALLISON P. COUDERT is the coauthor of four other books featuring Alice Whipple. She is also the author of a book on the history of alchemy and early chemistry. She teaches at Arizona State University in Tempe. She is married and has one daughter.

GIRL DETECTIVES HAVE MORE FUN!

From Bantam-Skylark Books
IT'S

From Betsy Haynes, the bestselling author of the Taffy Sinclair books, *The Great Mom Swap*, and *The Great Boyfriend Trap*, comes THE FABULOUS FIVE. Follow the adventures of Jana Morgan and the rest of THE FABULOUS FIVE as they begin the new school year in Wakeman Jr. High.

☐	SEVENTH-GRADE RUMORS (Book #1)	15625-X	$2.75
☐	THE TROUBLE WITH FLIRTING (Book #2)	15633-0	$2.75
☐	THE POPULARITY TRAP (Book #3)	15634-9	$2.75
☐	HER HONOR, KATIE SHANNON (Book #4)	15640-3	$2.75
☐	THE BRAGGING WAR (Book #5)	15651-9	$2.75
☐	THE PARENT GAME (Book #6)	15670-5	$2.75
☐	THE KISSING DISASTER (Book #7)	15710-8	$2.75
☐	THE RUNAWAY CRISIS (Book #8)	15719-1	$2.75
☐	THE BOYFRIEND DILEMMA (Book #9)	15720-5	$2.75
☐	PLAYING THE PART (Book #10)	15745-0	$2.75
☐	HIT AND RUN (Book #11)	15746-9	$2.75
☐	KATIE'S DATING TIPS (Book #12)	15748-5	$2.75
☐	THE CHRISTMAS COUNTDOWN (Book #13)	15756-6	$2.75
☐	SEVENTH-GRADE MENACE (Book #14)	15763-9	$2.75
☐	MELANIE'S IDENTITY CRISIS (Book #15)	15775-2	$2.75
☐	THE HOT-LINE EMERGENCY (Book #16)	15781-7	$2.75
☐	CELEBRITY AUCTION (Book #17)	15784-1	$2.75
☐	TEEN TAXI (Book #18)	15794-9	$2.75

Buy them at your local bookstore or use this page to order:

Bantam Books, Dept. SK28, 414 East Golf Road, Des Plaines, IL 60016

Please send me the items I have checked above. I am enclosing $_____ (please add $2.00 to cover postage and handling). Send check or money order, no cash or C.O.D.s please.

Mr/Ms _____ Virginia M. Tutt Branch

Address _____ 2223 Miami Street

City/State _____ South Bend, IN 46613

SK28-5/90

Please allow four to six weeks for delivery
Prices and availability subject to change without notice.